RESCUING RITA - A SANCTUM NOVEL

PEPPER NORTH

Cover Artist
ALLYSA HART

Pepper North
With a Wink Publishing, LLC

AUTHOR'S NOTE:

The following story is completely fictional. The characters are all over the age of 18 and as adults choose to live their lives in an age play environment. This is a series of books that can be read in any order. You may, however, choose to read them sequentially to enjoy the characters best. Subsequent books will feature characters that appear in previous novels as well as new faces.

OTHER TITLES BY PEPPER NORTH

The Magic of Twelve: Hazel

Roxy: Dr. Richards' Littles 21

Dr. Richards' Littles: First Anniversary Collection

Jillian: Dr. Richards' Littles 22

The Magic of Twelve: Sienna

Hunter: Dr. Richards' Littles 23

Sharing Shelby: A SANCTUM Novel

The Magic of Twelve: Pearl

Dr. Richards' Littles: MM Collection

Electrostatic Bonds

Grace: Dr. Richards' Littles 24

Looking After Lindy: A SANCTUM Novel

The Keepers: Naja

Tales from Zoey's Corner - ABC

Steven: Dr. Richards' Littles 25

The Magic of Twelve: Violet, Marigold, Hazel

The Magic of Twelve: Primrose

The Keepers Collection

Protecting Priscilla: A SANCTUM Novel

One Sweet Treat: A SANCTUM Novel

The Magic of Twelve: Sky

Sylvie: Dr. Richards' Littles 26

(appears in the Dirty Daddies Anniversary Anthology)

Tami: Dr. Richards' Littles 27

Liam: Dr. Richards' Littles 28

Dr. Richards' Littles: 2nd Anniversary Collection

Picking Poppy: A SANCTUM Novel

The Magic of Twelve: Amber

Tim: Dr. Richards' Littles 29

Once Upon A Time: A Dr. Richards' Littles Story

DEAR READERS,

I can't believe Rescuing Rita will be the sixth in the SANCTUM series. As the book releases, I'm listening to the audio tracks for Sharing Shelby, Looking After Lindy and Protecting Priscilla. They will be coming out in October of 2019 as a large combined audio set on Audible. I absolutely love hearing these books read aloud!

As I write this, I'm stacking up events to attend next year. If you've never been to a book conference or signing, you need to experience this fun! I'm trying to hit different parts of the states and have plans to travel outside the continental US in coming years. Let me know if you have a great event near you!

Hugs,

Pepper

CHAPTER 1

Margarita Alma sized up the pool hall as Eddie thrust her through the door. There were probably forty pool tables in organized rows around the large, open space. A long bar and a restaurant with a small gathering of tables completed the interior. Already, it was filled with people. Those that you would expect—tattooed men who would look perfectly at home on a motorcycle and those you wouldn't—friendly suburbanites who enjoyed a night out with friends.

Some people in that last group especially caught her eye. Not because they weren't hard looking. She'd run into all types of people in bars and pool halls during her bartending days. These individuals were in couples and triads. Still normal, but not. She could tell that some were in charge and dominant, while others followed their instructions, at least most of the time. All were having a blast learning how to play pool. One cute blonde even sat on her escort's lap as she enthusiastically encouraged the others.

Rita's eyes widened. They were Littles. That meant those people had to be Daddies and Mommies? Inside, her heart broke just a bit more. She'd been looking for her Daddy for a very long time.

She'd almost convinced herself that people didn't get to live in this special kind of relationship. That only the lucky characters in her books were able to enjoy having someone care for them so deeply. Now faced with proof that there were Daddies and Mommies out there, Rita couldn't help being jealous and sad even while she was in this crappy situation. Why did they get to have a Daddy, and she couldn't find one?

A rough hand shaking her arm forced her attention back to the present. She stared hard at the ugly man who gripped her upper arm. His fingers had tightened as he glared at her. "Remember. You say nothing! We're here to meet my … the buyer and then, we'll leave. Look happy!" he'd demanded when her face revealed just what she thought of him.

Rita despised this weasel of a man. Eddie Schaffer was the new owner of the bar she'd worked at for a couple of years. When he'd taken over two months ago, she had never trusted Eddie Schaffer. His long, thin face always looked like he was sucking on lemons. She was sure that there was no joy in his life. Now, standing in this pool hall, she knew he was up to no good.

Walking into the office earlier that night to give notice that she was quitting in two weeks, Rita had discovered him snorting a thin line of white powder. A plastic bag of a large quantity of the obvious drug sat on the desktop. Frozen in the doorway, Rita hadn't recovered fast enough to get herself out of there before Eddie pulled a gun from the desk. Scooping the drugs into a leather satchel, Eddie had forced her out the backdoor of the bar and into his car.

Under threat that he would shoot her and everyone around, Rita had cooperated. Now looking around at the Littles, Rita knew this wasn't the time to try to flee. She stood quietly with Eddie as he waited for someone that he was meeting there.

The curvy brunette knew he was nervous. Sweating bullets, Eddie was on his third beer. The bastard hadn't even been happy when the waitress brought her a glass of water when he wouldn't order anything for her. Nodding her thanks to the thoughtful server, Rita heeded the tightening grip on her arm, warning her not to say anything.

When his phone buzzed, Eddie set down his beer and looked at the screen with relief. Looking at Rita, he hissed quietly, "You stay here.

I'll be back in a minute. Don't try anything funny. I know where you live."

Nodding cooperatively, Rita took a sip of water to cover her immediate reaction. The moment he walked out that door, she would be out of here. With one last glare at her, Eddie released her arm. She watched him walk through the crowd. As soon as the pool players blocked her view, Rita turned and hurried to the restrooms.

Just as she hoped, there was an exit to the back parking lot. Rita darted through the door and froze. She could see Eddie standing behind the second row of cars talking to a scary-looking man. He hadn't seen her. Rita cursed the cute white and red top that she'd worn that night to work. It practically glowed in the dim light.

Moving as quickly as possible, Rita ducked between the cars to hide from the two men. Panic overwhelmed her thought processes as she focused on one word, escape. She didn't have a phone to call someone. Rita dropped her forehead against the nearest car. She had no credit cards to pay a cab or an Uber. It was a very long way back to her apartment, but even worse, Eddie knew where she lived. He had access to all her employment records as well as her purse that was tucked in its usual cubby under the bar.

The curvy brunette peeked over the car when she heard her name. The man Eddie had met wasn't happy.

"Why didn't you just shoot her on the way over?" he demanded.

"I'll take care of Rita later. She doesn't want anyone to get hurt. She'll follow my directions," Eddie tried to convince him.

"Bullshit! You're risking the whole operation. I'm going to jail because you can't remember to lock your office door. Go get her. I'll take her with me and get rid of the body," the threatening man directed.

Crap! She thought as she watched Eddie walk toward the rear door. He would discover that she was missing in just a few seconds and start looking for her.

An old-fashioned telephone ring sounded very close to Rita. *Double crap!* That scary-looking man was almost at her hiding spot. She heard him answer.

"What's she look like?" the man demanded, before directing, "Go look out front for her and then circle around to the back parking lot. She hasn't gotten away yet. I'll start looking back here."

Trying not to panic, Rita moved as quietly as possible to the last two cars parked in that row. Next to them, a large truck pulling a horse trailer was parked. In an open field next to the billiards house, a well-built man was slowly walking a large horse around. She couldn't help but scan his athletic body.

Cowboys definitely were nice to look at, she thought before panicking as she heard the footsteps of the man Eddie had met within the parking lot. Out of cars to hide behind, Rita ran to the closest shelter that she could find. Three quick steps and she was inside the horse trailer. Quickly, she ducked behind the barrier between the horse and the storage area at the far end of the trailer. Huddling behind the hay bales, she watched the shadowed entrance intently.

"Hey, cowboy!" the harsh voice spoke next to the open trailer.

"Yes? May I help you?" A warm, deep, masculine voice sounded from the other side of the lowered gate.

"Did you see a fat, dark-haired Hispanic woman running away out here? My missus and I had a misunderstanding. I'm trying to find her to apologize," the cretin answered.

Rita bristled at his description of her. She hated the word fat. She was curvy, but she'd still try to kick his butt if she wasn't sure that he had a gun. The thought of getting shot cooled her anger. Freezing where she was, Rita was confident that neither man knew where she was.

"I saw someone with dark hair headed toward that green car over there." The cowboy's voice had lost its warmth.

Hearing the scuff of the dangerous man's footsteps on the asphalt as he walked away, Rita breathed out a silent sigh of relief. To her horror, she heard the cowboy murmuring to the horse at the entrance of the trailer.

"Come on, Gumdrop. I should have known better than to stop here on a Friday night. Let's get you loaded up, and we can head to SANCTUM."

The voice was low and coaxing. Rita could hear the caring that this man had toward the giant horse. She cringed back against the hay bales as the man backed into the trailer, gently leading the animal inside.

What should she do? If she said something, the man could reveal her presence. They were obviously headed somewhere. The horse stepped his front feet into the trailer when she smelled Rita. Her flaring nostrils and the snort of distrust made the cowboy stop immediately.

"Whoa, girl. It's okay. What's wrong?" he asked the horse, plainly expecting her to answer him.

Charmed by the man's sweetness toward the mare, Rita took a chance. "Please, don't let that man know I'm here. They're going to kill me. I'm sorry I spooked your horse. I'm a good person. I promise," she whispered. Even she could hear the desperation in her voice.

"Whoa, Gumdrop. It's okay. I know you don't like the trailer," the man continued as if he hadn't heard her at all. Silently, he turned to search the darkness at the front of the trailer. His eyes spotted the cute, white stripes of her sailor top immediately.

In a low voice that Rita had to strain to hear, he directed, "Gumdrop won't come in with you here. Quietly, let yourself out the door to your left. The men are on the other side of the parking lot. My truck is open. Get in the passenger side and hide. Be careful as you get in. There's large metal pole extending through the cab on that side."

Without asking a single question, Rita quietly unlatched the door and snuck out. It took a bit of embarrassing wiggling because the door was narrow, and her bottom wasn't. She turned and relatched the door from the outside. Rita looked around the front of the trailer before crossing the gap between to get to the truck.

The last of her bravery was dissolving. Racing up the side of the large, heavy-duty truck, Rita eased open the door and jumped into the high seat. She missed the first time. Her legs were too short. She tumbled back to the ground, thankfully landing on her hands and feet.

Death by lack of athletic ability, she thought desperately. Lifting her foot again to the floorboard of the truck, Rita stretched upward to wrap her fingers around the grab bar above the window. With a determined lunge upward, the curvy young woman heaved herself up into the seat.

WHACK! Rita's temple bashed into something hard. Fortunately, her bottom slid into the deep seat, and she quickly closed the passenger door. She could hear the horse's feet clomping as she stepped into the trailer. Rita crossed her fingers that her impact with the bar had not been heard over that.

Shifting her body into the floor space of the big cab, Rita's shaking hand gently traced the rapidly swelling bump where the side of her head had crashed into the pole. She looked up to glare at the pole and immediately felt nauseous. Her eyes squeezed shut as she tried not to vomit.

Can this evening get any worse? She thought before trying to push that thought from her mind. With her luck tonight, it could.

CHAPTER 2

The slide of the two bolts seconds apart from each other told her that the cowboy had closed the trailer. Rita could hear the voices of the two men searching the parking lot getting louder. They were retracing their steps back toward this side of the parking lot.

She jumped when the driver's door opened. The interior light revealed the cowboy's handsome face. Rita's tension dropped. The man got in without looking at her at all. He pulled a large piece of fabric from that horrid bar over her seat and dropped it on top of her head, covering her body completely.

Starting the heavy-duty truck, he smoothly shifted it into gear and rolled forward gently so he didn't jerk Gumdrop behind them. The truck moved slowly down the drive on the far side of the pool hall and out onto the road. Rita held her breath that the men wouldn't suspect where she was.

Several minutes later, her savior announced, "It's safe to come out now." He pulled the blanket from over her head, dividing his attention between the road and glancing at her.

Rita moved in slow motion as she tried to convince herself that she was okay. Each shift in her position caused wave after wave of sickness to crash over her. Finally, she slid into the seat next to him with her hand over her mouth to keep herself from vomiting.

"Are you okay?" he asked, concerned.

"Sorry. You warned me, but I was too short to get into the truck, I jumped up but hit my head. It's thrown me for a loop. Thank you for helping me. I was in real trouble back there." Rita laid her head back against the seat and closed her eyes again. The glare of the on-coming cars aggravated her blooming headache.

"Little girl, I'm so sorry. You've had a bad evening," the man whispered as if reading her mind that everything was too loud.

"Little girl? If that's a fat joke, you can let me out right here," she demanded, leaning toward the door as if to jump out. Rita had been the brunt of mean girl vindictiveness in school when she couldn't get away from them. Now, she didn't put up with any unpleasantness.

His hand reached over to take her hand, tethering her in the car. "No. You will hurt or kill yourself. I will never say negative things about someone. That's not my way. I meant Little girl in another form. Not size but lifestyle."

Her growing headache made it hard to concentrate. Accepting his explanation, Rita couldn't think of the implication in his words. "Sorry. I'm Rita," she said, trying to keep it all together.

"Bart."

For some reason, his name made her smile. It fit this large cowboy perfectly. "Nice to meet you, Bartholomew.

"I'm worried about you, Rita. I'll head to the emergency room and let you out there. They can see if you've given yourself a concussion and bring in the police to address whatever was going on in that parking lot," he gently said.

"Do you have a last name?" He turned to smile at her before looking back at the traffic.

"Of course," Rita answered quickly. She searched for her last name and twisted her head to look at him, making herself sick again with the quick movement of her eyes.

As she took long slow breaths to calm her stomach, she tried to think of her last name. It dangled just outside her thoughts like something on the tip of your tongue. When she no longer risked throwing up, Rita admitted, "I don't know my last name. It's gone." She moved her head slowly to meet his eyes.

Worry filled her gaze. She didn't know what to do. Her head hurt so bad. "I don't think I remember a lot of things. I just bumped my head," she whispered.

CHAPTER 3

"Hold on, sweetheart. I'll get you to the hospital, and they'll fix you up." Bart pulled out his phone and selected a number.

"Jim, I need a favor. I have Gumdrop with me, and I'm on my way to SANCTUM. I need to stay here for a while. Could I borrow a stall in your barn for the night?" he asked. His eyes continued to jump from the road to the young woman next to him. He could tell that she was trying to hold it together but on the edge of panicking.

He cradled his phone between his ear and shoulder to reach a hand to the passenger side of the vehicle. At the feel of her icy cold hand, Bart wrapped his hand around her twisting fingers. At his touch, her fretting motions calmed.

Jim's voice brought his attention back to the call. Bart breathed a sigh of relief. "I owe you one, Jim," Bart said, thanking his friend.

Disconnecting the call, Bart slid his phone into his flannel shirt. "Okay. I found a place for Gumdrop for the night. I'm going to take you to the hospital and get you checked in. While they check you over, I'm going to take my mare and give her a nice place to sleep tonight. Then, I'll come back to check on you."

"You don't have to do that," she protested. "You don't even know me."

"I know you're Rita and that you need a Daddy," he answered

easily, squeezing her fingers before lifting his hand. "I know you're scared. I'm sorry the pole got you."

"Me, too," she admitted. "Could I hold your hand? I know it's silly, but it makes me feel less… lost."

Bart simply held out his hand to allow her to mesh her fingers with his. "That's why I'm here, Little girl. To make sure you feel better."

This time she didn't protest when he called her Little. Bart didn't know how he knew that she was a Little girl, he just did. The veterinarian had been looking for his own Little since he'd been in high school. Being a Daddy was just how he was wired. He'd enjoyed an age play relationship with a couple of women but hadn't ever found his one. Something in this curvy woman who needed him told him she could be his Little.

If nothing else, he wanted to make sure she was okay. The hospital would diagnose her with a severe concussion. He was sure her memory would come back, but that could take a while. The trauma of having those men after her followed by the blow to her head seemed to have wiped away her memory. Her mind had retreated to protect itself.

Squeezing her fingers before lifting his hand away, Bart turned into the hospital and parked the long trailer and truck at the back of the lot. He slid his six-foot three-inch frame from the cab and circled the front of the truck to open the passenger door. Taking care to avoid the metal rod that he had installed months ago to hold equipment and gear so he could grab it easily as he drove alone, Bart scooped her body into his arms.

Rita tried to wiggle from his arms, but he held her firmly in place. He could tell that even a slight movement to protest him carrying her had made her nauseous again. "Shhh, Little one. I will not drop you. You will always be safe with me," he promised her, looking down at her white face drawn with pain.

To his relief, she didn't protest any longer. Her big brown eyes simply closed. *She trusts me*, Bart thought with a slight smile breaking through the concern etched on his face.

Carrying her through the parking lot, Bart appreciated the soft feel of the beautiful woman in his arms. How anyone could want someone that was all bones and angles when they could have someone this voluptuous baffled him. She filled his arms to perfection.

Walking through the automatic doors into the emergency room, Bart placed her gently into a wheelchair. Her small sound of protest at leaving his arms struck him deeply. Steering her chair to the desk, he said, "This is Rita. She had a couple of men chasing her in the parking lot earlier this evening and then struck her head as she hid inside my truck. She's got a good size knot on her head and doesn't remember very much, other than her first name. I thought she needed to have someone make sure she's okay."

When the desk clerk tried to hand him a clipboard of papers to fill out, he waved them off. "I can't tell you anything other than her first name, and neither can she. Could we see the doctor, please?"

"Who are you?" the clerk asked with a snarl. The older woman didn't like puzzles or confusion. The look on her face revealed that she suspected that he might be the cause of the injury. If not, surely there was some information that he could provide.

"Hi, Doc! What are you doing here?" a friendly feminine voice drew his attention and that of the scornful desk attendant.

"Hi, Joanne! I brought in someone who needs some help. I was just explaining that I met Rita in a parking lot when two men were searching for her with obvious plans to hurt her. As I helped her escape, she jumped into my truck and struck her head on a metal bar. She can't remember anything now other than her first name. Could you help her?" Dr. Bartholomew Jennings asked the mom of one of his four-legged patients.

"We'll try our best. Peggy, wrap an orange amnesia wristband around Rita's wrist, and let's get her into a room so we can have a doctor look at her, stat," Joanne ordered as she took charge of the situation. She'd been an emergency room nurse for a lot of years. That pale, white look on Rita's face was enough to tell her that something was seriously wrong. Combined with her favorite vet's concern, she wasn't taking any chances with this patient.

"I have a new mare in my trailer outside. I'm going to take her to a friend's stable and then I'll be back. Will you add my name to Rita's records so I can get back in to see her?" Bart asked, torn between concern over Rita and the unfamiliar mare. He didn't want to see either one get hurt.

"Of course. Peggy, add Dr. Jennings to Rita's visitor's list." Joanne looked at Rita's white-knuckled grip on Bart's hand.

Squatting down to be at eye level, she said to Rita, "My name is Joanne. Dr. Jennings saved my five-week-old puppy when she ate something that she shouldn't have. I owe him one. I'm going to take as good of care of you as he did of Twinklebutt."

Standing to meet Bart's worried eyes, she said, "Go take care of that new horse. We'll be fine. If she can't remember anything, the police will want to talk to you."

"I'll be back in an hour," he promised.

The handsome man leaned over to whisper in Rita's ear, "As fast as I can, I will be right back. Be good, Little girl," he encouraged before kissing the back of the hand that clung to his.

Brown eyes opened to look at him. Squinting in the glare of the florescent bulbs that Bart knew would increase her headache, Rita looked at him as if memorizing his face. "I've wanted a Daddy for so long."

His heart skipped a beat. He was right. *She is a Little!* "We are going to talk about this when I get back, sweetheart. Don't forget me!" he ordered.

Her big brown eyes were filled with pain, but she tried to smile, "Never!"

Bart watched Joanne wheeled Rita back into the emergency room. He knew she'd take care of her. That didn't make it any easier to go take care of Gumdrop. He knew that he hadn't hurt her himself, but his stomach twisted in knots hoping that she wasn't seriously injured. Bart's gaze never left Rita until the emergency doors closed behind her, blocking his view.

CHAPTER 4

Joanne had helped Rita up onto the exam table. When she was lying comfortably, the kind nurse went to get an ice pack for her head and a warm blanket before starting to enter information into the computer. Logging her in as Rita Doe, Joanne signaled that the police needed to be informed that she was here.

Within a few minutes, an ER physician stopped by to check on the mysterious patient. Rita's throbbing head and faulty memory couldn't provide a lot of details. Rita tried to be brave, but her headache is so bad.

"I'm going to check your pupils, young lady. I'll be fast. I know this will be uncomfortable," the doctor says quietly. After a brief exam, he asks, "What's your name?"

"Rita," she whispers. Her voice is shaky.

"Tell me what happened," he asks.

"I think I hit my head, but I don't remember. I can't remember anything," she confessed. Big, fat tears welled from her eyes to roll down her cheeks. She was so frightened…and alone. Each time she opened her eyes, Rita hoped that she'd see Bart. In such a short time, she knew it was ridiculous, but she counted on him like her lifeline.

The doctor continued to ask questions. Rita did her best to remember but couldn't answer anything definitively. Finally, the doctor told her to rest when she could while they ran some tests. He didn't want to give her any pain medication until they determined whether she had a brain injury.

In the flurry of activity divided by brief quiet times, Rita endured being poked, prodded, and having all sorts of pictures taken of her skull. Through the whole thing, she hoped that on her next return to the small room in the ER that Bart would be there waiting for her. Each time, she was horribly disappointed to find the room empty.

The last time, she closed her eyes and allowed herself to sleep. Her dreams were tortured with two shadowy figures who pursued her. Rita knew that allowing these men to find her would be deadly. She jerked when a hand wrapped around her shoulder. Her body instinctively tried to flee, and she rolled away from that threatening touch. Her eyes shot open as she looked back at the man who had awakened her.

"Whoa, sweetheart! It's okay. It's just me. You were having a bad dream. I'm sorry for scaring you," Bart tried to reassure her.

"Bart? You're back?" Rita moved without thought as she rolled back to sit and throw herself into his arms. Her arms encircled his trim waist as she clung to him in desperation.

"Shhh!" Bart soothed the frightened woman with a tight hug before brushing his hands up and down Rita's spine.

Rita's heart beat ferociously inside her chest as she tried to recover from the scare. She forced herself to take several deep breaths as she willed him to continue to hold her close. After several minutes of listening to the steady throb of his heart against her cheek, Rita forced herself to talk. "Thank you for coming back," she whispered.

"You don't know me well, but you can be sure that I always keep my word," he assured her in a firm tone that helped Rita understand that this was his oath.

Nodding against his chest, Rita whispered, "I'm glad." She expected him to move away, but to her delight, he stayed close, allowing her to calm down.

"Are you doing okay?" he asked quietly after several minutes more.

"I still don't remember things. It's strange. I can remember my first name but I have no idea what my last name is. It's like my memory is swiss cheese. I can remember some things but there a whole bunch of holes. I don't know what I remember or don't until I try to think about something. It's really scary," she confessed. Her brown eyes glistened with unshed tears.

"I think that's probably normal. We'll see what the doctor says," he tried to reassure the Little girl.

A firm knock came on the door to the emergency treatment room. "Excuse me," a tall uniformed police officer said before continuing when the pair turned to look at him. "I'm Officer Doug Hamilton. I've been informed that you were injured tonight and needed to make a police report."

"Officer Hamilton," Bart acknowledged with a dip of his head. "I'm Bart Jennings, and this is Rita. We met tonight when Rita hid in my horse trailer to escape two men who were hunting her down in the Albertson Pool Hall."

"Sir, I'm going to ask you to step out of this room, please. I need to speak to Miss... Rita alone," the officer instructed firmly as his eyes assessed Bart for guilt in harming the attractive woman.

"What? No!" Rita protested, tightening her grip around Bart's waist.

The veterinarian simply dropped a kiss on her head before moving his hands around his back to unlatch her hold on him. "Rita, I'm not going anywhere. Let the policeman do his job to protect you. I'm going to step right out there," he said, pointing at the nurse's desk.

"But you just got back," she whispered. The tears that filled her eyes threatened to spill over onto her cheeks. She hadn't cried during this whole ordeal. She couldn't bear to have him leave again.

"I'm not going anywhere," he repeated as he stepped away. Nodding again to the police officer, Bart left the cubicle and walked across the hall, being careful to stay in Rita's line of sight.

"He didn't hurt me. Bart saved me," Rita said defensively to Officer Hamilton as he pulled a notebook and a pencil from his pocket.

"I understand, miss. It's just police procedure that I speak to you alone, first. Can you tell me your name?" The curvy, young woman's assurances did not sway the officer. He asked question after question as he tested the validity of her memory loss and tried to catch her in a lie.

After several minutes, Rita leaned back against her pillows once again. Her throbbing head ached, and she missed Bart. Still, she tried to answer the questions, but most of the answers eluded her. Some questions seemed silly, like where she grocery shopped or the color of her car. Others focused on the incident preceding her head injury.

Unfortunately, she didn't remember much. Just like the nightmare she had just dreamed, Rita was sure that two men had been after her. She didn't know why, and she didn't know their names, nor could she describe them. The menace scared her still, her pulse racing as she struggled to remember the details.

Finally, the police officer motioned Bart back into the room and asked him what information he could give. His eyes watched their interaction closely. Officer Hamilton had interviewed many women who he'd known were abused partners in a relationship. He did not get that vibe from these two. Pushing that from his mind, he focused on getting as much information as possible.

"I stopped at the field next to the pool hall to allow my new mare to have a break from the trailer. I bought her at the Thompson Stables this morning and was transporting her to my property to the west. One man talked to me, asking if I'd seen a Hispanic woman and claiming that she was his angry wife who'd left the bar. He was not very complimentary," Bart said with a sideways glance at Rita, who lie with her eyes closed. When his eyes met the police officers, there was visible anger in his gaze.

"What did he look like?" the officer demanded.

"The man I spoke with was shorter than me-probably just under six feet. He had brown hair and dark eyes. The edge of the parking lot wasn't well lit. Average build. His demeanor was threatening-not to me, but toward the lady he was looking for. I saw him on the other side of the lot where it was lighter, that's how I know he had brown hair. He was talking to another man who was dressed more professionally than the man I talked to. He was wearing khakis and a blue polo shirt. There was some logo on the pocket of the polo, but he was too far away for me to see it."

Rita's eyes opened, and she sat up slightly before shaking her head. She almost remembered something she knew was important. Her left hand rose to press lightly against the swelling on her head. The nausea that resulted from moving her head seemed to decrease, but the pain seemed to fill her mind, preventing her from thinking.

"Did you remember something, miss?" the police officer asked quickly.

"I'm sorry. I thought I remembered something but it's just not coming to me. I hate this," Rita answered with a frown.

"I think that's all of my questions," he said as he reached into his pocket for a card to leave with each of them. "Here's my contact information. Please call me if you remember anything. Leave a message if I don't answer. I'll get back to you as quickly as possible. I'll need your contact information. Mr. Jennings."

Joanne bustled into the room with a fresh ice pack for Rita. "It's Dr. Jennings, Doug. He's the best veterinarian around," she added to clarify the type of doctor that Bart was. "I just wish he wasn't only going to be working part time now."

The policeman's stance relaxed a bit more. He'd worked with Joanne several times in the past when he'd interviewed someone in the hospital. He obviously knew that she was a good judge of character. "Dr. Jennings?" he asked, correcting himself.

Bart provided his cellphone number and his address in town. His hand brushed through Rita's richly dark brown hair, carefully avoiding her injury. "I'll let you know immediately if she remembers anything."

Rita's eyes closed in the enjoyment of Bart's caress. Without thinking, she rattled off a phone number. Her eyes blinked open in surprise. Everyone was looking at her with a shocked expression except for Officer Hamilton, who quickly finished jotting down the numbers.

Everyone watched as he pulled out his phone and entered the number. He tilted the phone so that everyone could hear the tones that signaled a disconnected number. "I'll do some research. I have a feeling that's not your current number but a phone number from your past—maybe your childhood. It's a clue to help us. I'll also check the missing persons listing. There's no one matching your description on the list now." He quickly took a picture of Rita.

The flash made her eyes water in pain. She pressed the fresh ice pack to her head more firmly. Nodding slightly as he apologized, Rita closed her eyes and clung to Bart's hand. She missed the officer's departure from the room.

CHAPTER 5

In a flurry of activity, the emergency room doctor returned to share the results of the testing along with a nurse that brought in a pain reliever just slightly more potent than an over-the-counter drug. The doctor introduced himself to Bart while the unfamiliar nurse raised the head of Rita's bed higher and helped her take the medicine. When she had swallowed the pill, the doctor opened her chart and reviewed the findings.

Speaking to Bart, he said, "I understand that you were with her when she suffered the head injury? Do you know anything about Rita's medical history?"

When the veterinarian shook his head no, the doctor continued, "There is no sign of swelling of the brain tissue. This is an excellent sign. Because of the memory loss and Rita's other symptoms, it's clear that she has a serious concussion. She will need care and supervision while she recovers. Will you be able to stay with her?"

"I'm going to take her with me with your okay. I have a country home that I was headed to when we met," Bart informed the physician.

Rita watched him carefully. She didn't want to be a burden. She opened her mouth to volunteer that she could take care of herself, but she realized she had no idea where to go. The thought of those shadowy figures flashed into her mind, and she slid her hand into Bart's. He quickly reassured her with a squeeze of his fingers as the doctor continued.

"Since we are unsure of her primary care physician, I will count on your medical skills to note if she has concerning signs such as a worsening headache or confusion. Wake her up, every three hours at least, to make sure that you can rouse her easily. For her headache, treat with ice, on and off and stay away from aspirin-based pain relievers. Those could cause bleeding in the brain. Consult a physician or bring Rita back to the hospital if her symptoms worsen," the doctor advised.

He looked at Rita and cautioned her, "You'll feel bad for several days. Don't do too much physically or mentally. Be mindful of what your body and mind are telling you. Don't push yourself, or you'll delay your recovery."

Pausing to choose his words carefully, the doctor glanced over at Bart and then back at Rita. "Your recovery could be very frustrating. The amnesia could disappear in three hours or three months, maybe longer. Your brain is in charge. You may regain chunks of memories or strange bits of information may appear. There's no way to rush it."

"I'll make sure she takes it easy, doctor," Bart said as he squeezed her fingers once again before letting go of her hand to shake the doctor's and thank him for taking care of Rita.

Joanne walked in with several pieces of paper. "I've got all the recommendations for dealing with a concussion here. When you sign these papers, you'll be free to go."

CHAPTER 6

B art hurried to the far end of the parking lot to retrieve his truck and trailer in the early dawn light. Driving to the front of the hospital, he jumped out to lift Rita from the wheelchair that Joanne had required her to ride in as they exited the emergency room. When she tried to fuss that she was too heavy, he was already placing her into the passenger seat without any sign of distress or struggle. Bart patted her leg and leaned across her to fasten her seatbelt.

When Rita looked up cautiously for the bar that had hung over her head, it surprised her to find that it was no longer there. She smiled at Bart as he slid into the driver's seat before apologizing, "I'm sorry that you're stuck with me. You could drop me off at a hotel ..." she began before the smile slid from her lips as she realized that she had no money or credit cards to pay for a room. The reality of her situation crashed over her. What was she going to do?

"You're going to stay with me where I can keep an eye on your health and make sure you're protected from harm." Bart's voice left no wiggle room for her to deny his assertion.

"Are you sure?" she asked in a small, quivering voice.

"I found you. I'm keeping you," he announced with a smile before laughing and lightening the mood. "Well, Gumdrop found you."

A companionable silence fell over the cab. Rita peeked over at Bart after several minutes. "Aren't you going to feel strange riding a horse named Gumdrop?" she asked with a smirk.

"Gumdrop is for my Little girl."

"Oh," she answered in a tiny voice. Rita's heart sank. Deep inside her, she knew that she'd been looking for a Daddy for a long time. Now, she'd found one but, he already had a Little girl. Trying to figure out what to do, Rita was still debating when Bart pulled into a driveway, passing a farmhouse to drive to the large barn.

"Do you want to go into the barn with me, Little girl, or do you want to stay here and rest?" Bart asked, looking at her as he turned off the truck.

Thinking fast, Rita answered, "I'll just stay here and see if I can go to sleep. My head will feel better after I sleep for a while." She knew that she would need to disappear to allow Bart to be with his Little.

"It's been a long time since we've both eaten, I guess. Are you hungry?" Bart asked, reaching past her knees to remove a box of protein bars from the glove box. When her stomach growled in response, he pulled out one individually wrapped packet and opened it for her. "Here, eat one of these."

Bart inhaled his bar quickly and watched her take a tentative bite from hers. He smiled as she quickly chewed and took a bigger bite before saying. "They're good, aren't they? Have another bar or two if you're hungry. I'll go unload Gumdrop. I'll be back as soon as I get her loaded in the back."

Hearing Gumdrop's name made Rita remember that Bart already had a Little girl and couldn't be her Daddy. Her eyes dropped to the almost finished bar in front of her. *If only Bart could still be looking for his Little girl*, Rita thought sadly. Quickly, she covered her thoughts by saying, "Be careful. Tell Gumdrop hello for me." She popped the last morsel into her mouth to keep from blurting out anything else.

Bart nodded and slid from behind the wheel. He surprised her by rounding the hood of the truck, and instead of heading into the barn, the kind man opened her door. "If you're finished eating, let's lay your seat back so you can be comfortable," he murmured as he operated a lever to lower her seatback.

Closing her door, Bart opened the back door into the extended cab to reach into the back of the seat. He leaned over her to pull the blanket from its new storage place. The smaller segments of the rod that had extended over her head clinked together.

His position stretched across her body brought his lips close to her. Unable to stop, Rita licked her naturally red lips as his drew her attention. Her eyes flew to meet his when a deep groan sounded in his throat.

"Little girl, you may be the death of me," he said, his deep voice sounding even lower, guiltily drawing her attention to his face seconds before his lips took hers.

It was not a soft, introductory kiss. Bart's lips pressed hers apart as if it was his right to kiss her. Her soft gasp of delight only allowed him freer access to the interior of her mouth as his tongue swept in to meet hers. He did not allow her to remain passive but drew a response from her.

Rita couldn't resist the delight of his kiss. Eagerly, she pressed her mouth to his savoring the masculine, clean flavor that was simply his. Her arms looped around his neck as she arched from the reclined seat to press her torso against his. She wished that this moment would never end and protested with a low whining sound as he raised his lips just enough to break their contact.

"Oh, Little girl, how you make me forget that I'm supposed to be taking care of you, not kissing the breath from you," Bart murmured against her lips.

"Please!" she begged, holding her breath. To her delight, his lips pressed against hers once again. Avoiding the bump on the side of her head, Bart threaded his fingers through her thick brown hair and tugged slightly, drawing her attention from her injury and sending an erotic thrill down her spine. All thoughts fled from her mind as she focused on the feel of his mouth seducing her.

A low sound of disappointment slipped from her when his lips rose from hers, and his body lifted away from Rita. After spreading the blanket over her body, Bart stopped to look at her before cupping her chin. He tilted her eyes up to meet his and said, "Sleep, Little girl. I'll load Gumdrop, and I'll be right back."

Her heart sank as he stepped back to close the door, enclosing her in the cab. She heard him lower the gate on the trailer before she saw him enter the large building. His words reminded her he already had a Little girl and had even bought Gumdrop for her. She was sure that horses were expensive and required a lot of attention and care for years. Buying one for someone was a sign of a lasting commitment. He was already taken. She wasn't the type to mess with someone who was already in a committed relationship. That wasn't fair to anyone involved.

Rita knew what she needed to do. When he disappeared into the barn, Rita forced her body to sit back up in the chair. Shoving the blanket to the side, she turned quickly to find the door latch. Her hand tightly gripped the armrest as she was forced to pause for the dizziness to subside.

When her eyes would focus once again, Rita tried to find a balance between moving too rapidly and making herself dizzy. She needed to flee while Bart was still occupied in the barn. She didn't know who his Little was, but she'd been lucky enough to find her Daddy. Rita didn't want to interfere.

Sliding from the tall cab seemed like a mile-long drop. The impact of her feet striking the ground took her breath away, and she gripped the door. Panting as her brain seemed to slosh around inside her skull. Dizzy and not able to focus well, Rita forced herself to step away from the cab and push the door closed as quietly as possible.

She rested her hand against the cool metal of the truck and made herself move around the front of the vehicle. Rita had just reached the driver's side when she heard the jingle of Gumdrop's reins. Leaning down slightly to hide behind the tall truck, she waited until she heard Bart patiently encouraging Gumdrop to climb the ramp into the trailer and heard the horse's feet step up on the metal floor.

Hurrying as fast as she could, Rita walked unsteadily toward the woods that lined the long drive. She didn't want Bart to feel burdened by her or responsible for taking care of her. Her fingers rose to press against her lips. She hoped someday if she was lucky enough to find her Daddy that he was just like Bart.

Her eyes closed briefly as tears overwhelmed her vision. She'd been too late to find the kind man. He belonged to some other Little.

"Where did you come from, darling?" a rough voice asked from the side.

Rita turned to look at an older man with silvery hair. His lean muscled body filled his worn jeans and a denim jacket. She tried to come up with a good story, but her head was pounding. Her hand automatically went to her injury as she tried to soothe away the pain.

"Did you ride in with Bart, honey?" he asked. When she looked at him in confusion, trying to come up with a story, he walked forward to wrap an arm around her. "Are you hurt? You look like you're about ready to drop in your tracks. Let's go talk to my buddy, Bart. I don't want him to think I'm poaching his girl."

"He already has a Little girl," Rita blurted out as she leaned against this friendly stranger for support.

The older man's blue eyes softened, and he looked at the curvy woman tucked next to him. "I think we need to talk to Bart even more. Bart has been searching for his Little for a long time. I suspect he may think he's met her now."

"I know. I just need to go," Rita confessed. The tears that had been threatening began to roll down her cheeks. Crying only made her head hurt more. She tried to stop as she brushed the tears away, but they just kept falling.

"Rita? What are you doing outside the truck? Did you need to go to the restroom?" A familiar voice sounded close to her. She turned her head to watch the handsome man finish covering the distance that separated them.

"I was worried about her, Bart. She didn't seem to move well." As Bart reached them, the older man continued, "She is upset. I believe she thinks you have a Little girl and that she should go." He stepped back to allow Bart to take his place supporting the brunette.

"I'll just go. I'll be okay. I'm sorry I've delayed your Little getting to meet Gumdrop." Rita tried to step away from the man who had saved her, but he tightened his arm around her waist, holding her next to him. Futilely, she resisted as Bart turned her to face at him. Her eyes dropped to the dirt under her once white sneakers.

When he dropped to his knees, her eyes flew to meet his. "I think you misunderstood, Rita. I bought Gumdrop so that whenever I was lucky enough to find my Little girl, she would have a horse to ride. I didn't have a Little girl before I met you," he stressed, running a large hand over her cheek and threading his fingers back into her hair on the uninjured side of her head. "I didn't know that buying Gumdrop would help me find a Little girl who I hope will turn out to be mine."

Stepping forward into his arms, Rita collapsed against his muscular body. This time, she didn't protest when he stood, and his arms looped under the curve of her bottom to lift her into his arms. She laid her head on his shoulder in relief as her mind stopped whirling in panic. Bart would take care of everything.

"Thanks, Dirk. I appreciate you making sure that Rita was okay and keeping her from running away before I could explain my words. She's had a very hard last few hours. I'm taking her to SANCTUM with me to recover from her head injury. I owe you one for looking after Gumdrop for me," he said with a smile.

"I'll take you up on that one when I come to visit. You take care of Rita, or I may just try to steal her away," he joked. His eyes twinkled when her arms tightened visibly around Bart's neck. "Or better yet, I'll just find my Little girl, and they can be friends. Come on. Let me open the door for you if you've got Gumdrop settled."

In only a few minutes, the trio of a new mare and a handsome man with an exhausted Little girl stretched out with her head on his thigh set off down the driveway back to the highway. His strong, skilled hand wrapped around her shoulder as one of her hands clung to his leg under her cheek. Only then did Rita allow herself to sleep.

CHAPTER 7

Bart was used to missing a night's sleep. Animals needing assistance came at all hours of the day and night. As he negotiated the secured entrance into SANCTUM, he watched Rita carefully. She had slept the entire morning as he drove to the remote community, plagued by bad dreams twice. To his relief, Rita had settled back into more pleasant sleep when he'd rubbed her back and softly reassured her.

Rita murmured sleepily as Bart brushed his warm hand over her shoulder and down her arm to rouse her. His blue eyes watched her carefully as he tried to assess how easily he could wake her. Concussions could be very serious. Her memory loss alone concerned him. To his relief, her big, brown eyes blinked opened and her hand tightened around his thigh.

Inwardly, Bart groaned as her fingers bit into his tense muscles. After he tilted his steering wheel up as high as possible when they'd first set out, Rita had settled into a more comfortable position with her head resting high on his leg, nestled against his pelvis. As she slept, Bart had felt her warm breath puff through the denim stretching tightly over his muscular leg. Other parts of his jeans had become tighter with each mile that they passed.

"Bart?" she asked sleepily before realizing just how intimately she was nestled against him. She pushed against his thigh to press up to sitting but swayed when the sudden motion seemed to make her dizzy.

His arm wrapped around her to steady her body. "Whoa, Little girl. You need to move slowly, okay?"

She leaned against him as those brown eyes closed in discomfort. "I'm really tired of my head feeling like this already," she complained.

"I know. It will get better," he reassured her.

"Do you think?" Rita asked, opening her eyes to scrutinize his expression.

"Yes," Bart confidently answered. The veterinarian knew that amnesia could be a lingering ailment. There was no timetable for memories to return. The worst thing to do was to try to force them back. That never worked. He needed to keep her hopeful and relaxed to aid the process. He hated to admit even to himself that he hoped that regaining her memories would take a while. Already, he wanted to keep her with him.

Her eyes drifted past him to see a wide-open green space surrounding them. "We've stopped. Are we wherever you were planning to go?" she asked, moving her head slowly to look around. Behind her, she saw a large red barn with an open double-wide door. "Is this where Gumdrop will stay?"

"Yes. This is the barn we constructed to house our shared equipment, supplies, and horses. Come on. You can help me show Gumdrop her new home as you stretch your legs a bit. Stay right there. I'll come to help you out," Bart instructed before opening his door.

Before he had rounded the front of the vehicle, Rita opened her door. "Little girl, wait right there," he sternly called. When she hesitated and didn't try to slide from the truck, Bart controlled the smile that wanted to spread over his lips. *She responds instantly to a dominant voice.* It was just one more clue that she needed to have a Daddy to take care of her.

As he approached the open door, Bart's large hands spanned each plump thigh to hold her in place as he looked at her solemnly. "You need to follow my directions, completely and immediately, Rita. I am here to take care of you. If I tell you to wait, wait. By opening your door and getting ready to jump out on your own when I've implicitly instructed you to stay where you are, you chose to be disobedient. Disobedience earns a Little girl a spanking." He watched her eyes widen. I won't spank you today because of your injury, but there are many ways a Daddy can punish his Little for not following directions. Do you understand?"

Again, he had to control his expression as he felt her thighs contract under his grip as she squeezed her legs together when he warned her of a spanking and again as he hinted at possible punishments. His Little was aroused by the thought of consequences that he would dole out. *His Little,* he thought to himself, realizing just how strongly he cared for this precious young woman. His mind had already claimed her.

Without another word, Bart wrapped his hands around her waist and lifted her from the truck. Setting her gently on the ground, he took her hand and led her to the back of the trailer. "Will you do me a favor?" he asked.

"Yes," she eagerly answered.

As he thought, Rita needed to feel like she was doing something to repay the care he was giving her. The Little obviously didn't want to feel like she was imposing. Little did she know that he was only too glad to take care of the enticing woman who had hidden in his trailer.

"I'm going to open the door. You hold it against the side here, so it doesn't slam shut on Gumdrop and me. I don't want her to spook. Do not move in front of the trailer ramp. The mare is a bit skittish because she's in a new environment," he warned.

"Okay. I promise," Rita answered in a small voice that revealed her curiosity and slight fear of the beautiful mare that he had purchased.

"Thank you," he said as he opened the lock and pulled the door open. Pressing the door to the side of the trailer, he showed her how to hold it in place, ensuring that her body would stay to the side out of the way.

Talking gently to the mare, Bart walked slowly past her flank to caress her long elegant neck. Gumdrop was a beauty. Calm and placid with a desire to please, the mare was precisely what he had been looking for as a mount for his Little. Even though he hadn't found his, Bart had purchased Gumdrop without a qualm. The other Littles in SANCTUM would enjoy riding her. Now, his fingers were crossed in the hope that by the time it was safe for Rita to horseback ride, that the horse would have a permanent rider.

Bart patiently urged Gumdrop backward. This was a leap of faith for the horse to step into empty space. Would she trust him that it was safe? With only a slight hesitation, the mare lowered one foot to the ground. Reassured, she stepped quickly from the trailer.

He allowed her to look around and sniff the air as Gumdrop assessed her new home. Tossing her mane, Gumdrop nudged his shoulder with her soft nose. Bart laughed softly.

"Can I come over?" Rita asked from her position next to the trailer.

"Sure, honey. Just walk around the back of the trailer and come behind me to stand on my left," he continued to stroke Gumdrop's neck as he watched Rita follow his directions completely.

When she was at his side, Bart held out one palm for her hand. "Let her smell you a moment, and then you can pet her nose," he instructed as he guided her to accomplish those tasks.

"She's so soft!" Rita whispered, emphatically before giggling as Gumdrop snorted against her palm.

"She likes you," Bart said with a smile.

"I like her, too." Rita looked at him with stars in her eyes.

Bart's heart lurched slightly inside his chest. It was the first real smile that he'd received. *My Rita is so beautiful.* He dropped his hand and wrapped it around her waist from the back to pull her gently to his side. "I'm glad. Let's show, Gumdrop, where she'll be sleeping."

Leading Gumdrop into the barn, he paused to allow the mare to look around and scent the other horses that lived inside. Bart pointed to a large white jar sitting on one of the railings. "Go get Gumdrop a treat. There are sugar cubes in that white cannister. Get one and meet me at Gumdrop's stall. Don't come in until I tell you that it's safe," he warned.

He watched Rita slowly walk toward the jar. Confident that she was learning to move sedately to avoid making her head ache more, Bart turned around to lead the horse to an empty stall. The sweet mare had surprised him with her adaptability and pleasant demeanor.

The only time she had refused to do anything had been when Rita had hidden in the trailer. Horses saw much better in the darkness than humans did. Gumdrop hadn't panicked. She had just hesitated, uncertain about the unexpected person at the end of the trailer.

Closing the stall door behind him, Bart ran an admiring hand down the goldish brown horse's sleek coat. Shiny and glowing with health, Bart had known he would buy her immediately. Unfastening her bridle, Bart talked quietly to the horse. It didn't matter what his words were, she just needed to become accustomed to his voice. The pretty mare's ears turned toward him as Bart told her about all the other horses in the barn.

A slight noise at the gate made them both turn to look at the Little reaching a hand over with two sugar lumps extended. Gumdrop immediately lifted her nose as she sniffed the air. Bart stepped back as she curiously turned to approach the offering.

"One sugar lump at a time," Bart warned. Immediately, Rita obediently plucked one cube from her palm and held it behind her back. Gumdrop snorted as if she was ticked that one of the treats had disappeared.

"It's his fault, Gumdrop. Come try this one, and then I'll sneak you the second one when he's not watching," Rita confided to the mare. A huge smile spread across her lips as the horse walked forward to pluck the cube daintily from the young woman's outstretched palm.

Bart smiled at the giggles that bubbled from Rita's mouth as the horse's soft muzzle, brushed against her palm. For a moment, the horse distracted Rita from her pain and worries. When Gumdrop nuzzled her hand looking for another treat, magically, another cube appeared on her palm. The horse quickly disposed of that one as well.

"You're going to spoil her," Bart warned with a laugh. He was pleased to see that Rita seemed unafraid of the mare. From her tentative motions to pet the horse's long neck, he could tell that being around the large four-legged creatures was new to her.

"Everyone needs a bit of spoiling," Rita answered automatically. Her eyes were fixed on the mare.

As Gumdrop and Rita became acquainted, Bart moved quietly around the stall to fill Gumdrop's water and put oats and hay into her feed bin. Only the sound of the sweet oats being added for her to eat tempted the gentle horse away from her new friend.

"Come on, Little girl. Gumdrop's all set now. Let's get you settled as well," Bart announced as he took her hand and led Rita from the stall. She followed him slowly. He could tell she didn't want to leave, but she was as tired as he suspected. The nap in the car hadn't satisfied her need to begin to recover from the head injury.

Lifting her back into the passenger seat, Bart secured her seatbelt before closing the door. Thank goodness his house was finished now. He'd get her settled for a nap before checking to see if the police officer had made any progress in determining who she was.

CHAPTER 8

Pushing her forearm against the soft mattress to look around, Rita's sleepy eyes widened at her surroundings. She was in a dreamy room with light purple walls. She smiled and sat up fully at the sight of an enormous rainbow-sherbet colored unicorn that filled one wall. Rita swayed a little as the movement made her slightly dizzy. She felt slightly better than before, but she definitely had messed up her head.

She moved more cautiously as she tried to understand the room that she was in. Rita had never seen anything like this. *It looks like a nursery, but...* Suddenly, she realized this was a nursery, only sized for an adult. Bart really had been looking for his Little girl. He'd even created this room for her.

Her hands lifted to wrap around the bars in front of her. She was sitting in a crib. Rattling the bars slightly to test whether she could lower them, Rita's heart beat a bit faster as she figured out that Bart would have to release her.

Hesitant to call out, she looked around the room. Over there stood a large padded rocking chair. It had a small table next to it with several drawers. A sizable flat table with a padded top sat across the room from her. There seemed to be all sorts of supplies handily arranged under and next to the cushioned section. A large chest sat against the other wall with an over-sized, stuffed zebra on top. Rita smiled at the pink polka-dotted bow tied around its neck.

"Hi, honey. Did you wake up from your nap?" a warm voice from the side drew her attention away from the stuffed animal.

"Hi!" she shyly answered, looking down at the bright yellow blanket that still covered her legs. "I'm sorry I fell asleep again. I don't remember coming in here."

"Nope. You were out the minute that the truck started moving. That's a good thing. Your body needed sleep. How do you like your room, honey?" Bart asked.

She stared at him for several seconds, trying to quell the hope that welled inside of her. Could she really have a chance to be a Little girl? She almost hated to dare think her dreams could come true. Her big brown eyes met his as she struggled with what to say.

"Little girl," he answered the uncertainty and fright that she knew showed in her eyes.

Walking forward to stand in front of the crib, Bart triggered something below her with his foot, releasing the railing to slide down in front of her. His arms reached in to pluck her from the mattress and cuddle her against his body. He rocked her gently in his arms for several seconds as her arms automatically reached up to encircle his neck.

When he turned to stride toward the rocking chair she had spotted earlier, Rita's arms tightened around his neck. "I can walk," she whispered into his ear. She knew that she was heavy. Rita had always struggled with her weight. She'd given up on dieting because each time she tried to lose the extra pounds, she'd ended up gaining more when the diet was over. Now, she just tried to eat healthy foods and get some exercise. She was embarrassed to have Bart carry her.

"I enjoy holding you in my arms," he answered and pressed a kiss to her forehead. Bart sat in the large rocking chair with her tucked securely into his arms.

"I'm too heavy to carry around," she protested, hiding her face against his shoulder. She didn't want to talk about her weight but would feel horrible if he hurt himself.

"How about if you let me decide whether I wish to carry you?

Sometimes a Daddy just needs to feel his Little in his arms," Bart informed her as he lifted her chin

"I don't want you to strain your back," she whispered as her face heated, revealing a bright red blush to him.

"I promise you I won't hurt myself if you promise me you'll try to trust your Daddy," Bart said with a solemn look.

"You're not my Daddy. I don't have a Daddy," she protested in a small voice.

"I'm officially applying for the job," he answered with a smile.

When he didn't say anything other than stating his intentions, Rita hesitated and then finally answered, "You don't really know me. I don't even know who I am. I could be a horrible person."

Bart's smile never wavered. If anything, his lips tilted up just a bit more. "I know you're not a horrible person. Losing your memory doesn't change who you are. Your injury simply magnifies your personality," he told her as he began to rock the chair under them.

"I don't feel like a bad person," she quietly answered.

"Will you let me show you what it would be like to be my Little while you recover here?" Bart asked, holding her eyes captive with his blue ones.

Rita waged a battle in her head. She wanted to have a Daddy. But Bart was so attractive. There was no way that he really wanted her to be his Little. She was too ordinary. Her eyes closed as her head began to hurt once again.

Something brushed against her lower lip. Automatically, she opened her mouth as her eyes opened as well. "Drink, Little girl. I know you don't trust me yet, but I'm not going away. How about if I take care of you for as long as you'll let me?" he proposed as he pressed the bottle's nipple between her pink lips.

When she tentatively sucked on the large nipple filling her mouth, a wave of fresh water filled her mouth. Realizing that she was extremely thirsty, Rita continued to pull the cool liquid from the bottle. She swallowed eagerly as Bart continued to rock them slowly in the comfortable chair.

When she finished the bottle, Bart set it on the table next to them and continued to rock. His fingers brushed through her hair, being

37

careful to avoid the left side that had struck the bar. Her eyes closed in contentment at his caresses, soothed by the warmth surrounding her as he held her cradled in his arms.

"Little girl, you rest for a few minutes, and then we'll get something in your tummy," he said softly after a long pause. "I've searched for my Little girl for a long time. I knew that when I met her, I would know immediately. It didn't matter what she looked like, but in my mind, I always pictured her with big brown eyes and long, brunette hair that begged to be tugged." His fingers tangled in the strands of her silky hair to pull gently.

"Oh!" popped from her mouth as she felt that pull on her scalp vibrate down her body to kindle the heat in her belly.

"I know, Little girl. I respond to your touch, as well. That's how I know that you're mine," he said in a growly voice that made her look at him in surprise.

The look of desire on his face made her heart skip a beat. No one had ever looked at her that way. Like she was something so desirous that he could barely keep his hands from exploring her body. "Daddy?" she whispered.

"Yes, Little girl. I'm glad you feel it, too." Bart sat her up to sit on his lap, and he pulled her in for a quick kiss. "Time to eat, Ritagirl. The last two words he slurred together as if they were one.

She smiled at him. She liked that name. It seemed to combine both parts of her, the Little girl that she'd always dreamed of being and the only name she could remember for herself. Her adult self and her Little side combined at last.

CHAPTER 9

Rita felt silly sitting in the adult-sized high chair at the table. Used to chairs fitting snuggly around her plump bottom, the Little squirmed on the wide wooden seat and pushed against the tray fixed tightly in front of her. She felt even more Little as she watched Bart prepare a few sandwiches for the two of them. Her fingers chased a few grapes around the tray as her mind tried to acclimate to the elevated seat.

Her feet swinging in midair, she tried to push the tray away stealthily for a second time. It didn't budge. Staring at the tray in frustration, Rita popped a grape into her mouth. The crisp, sweet flavor burst through her mouth. "Mmmm!" she murmured, wiggling in her chair once again.

Freezing as Bart dropped a kiss carefully on the right side of her head away from the injury, Rita peeked up at him. She wasn't sure what she was supposed to do. *Was there a wrong way to be Little?* she wondered.

"Eating grapes are loads more fun than trying to unlatch the tray. I've made sure that you're secure, so you don't fall out and hurt yourself. You don't need to hit the other side of your head. It's a long way down for a Little girl to fall," he said, gesturing down to the tiled floor below.

The floor did look far away when she peered over the tray. Reassured that he was taking care of her and not penning her in place, Rita smiled at him. She laughed when Bart theatrically grabbed his heart and dropped to one knee next to the highchair. "You're silly, Bart... um, Daddy."

"That, Ritagirl, is the first true smile that I've seen on your pretty face," he leaned forward to capture her lips once again. The heat that she'd experienced from his previous kisses flamed between them once again.

Her hand reached out to gather the soft material of his shirt into her grip, pulling herself closer to the handsome man's skilled lips. His tongue explored the inside of her mouth. He invited her to participate, but he was in charge. Rita thrilled at the feeling of his dominance as his lips and tongue tasted and tantalized her.

When he lifted his mouth away from hers, Rita panted breathlessly. She'd forgotten to breathe as he kissed her. Bemused, her hand lifted from his shirt to trace her swollen lips.

"Ritagirl, you call me anything you want. I hope someday you'll call me Daddy without any reservations. For now, there's no pressure. I'll just keep trying my best to woo my Little girl. Okay?" he asked, fondly smiling at her as his hand brushed the hair from her eyes.

"Okay," she whispered.

"All these sweet kisses and I haven't fed you yet. Let's eat before we both perish from lack of nutrition. Then, it's a bath and bed for you," he announced as he stood and grabbed the plate from the kitchen counter.

Bart set half of a thick sandwich in front of her. Then, he turned to grab the milk from the fridge and pour it into a glass and a small plastic cup. Setting it back into the cooled chamber, he snapped a sippy lid on top of the cup and placed it on her tray. "It's a good thing that I asked Josiah and Lindy to add a few items to their grocery list this week. We would have been begging for food from the neighbors."

"Where are we?" she asked before taking a big bite of the sandwich and wiggling in delight on the high wooden seat below her bottom. The delicious taste made her realize just how hungry she was. She looked around, moving her head carefully to avoid making herself dizzy as she checked the time. Six o'clock! That had to be in the evening. No wonder she was hungry!

"We're in SANCTUM," he answered, watching her closely.

"What's SANCTUM?" she asked before taking another big bite from the sandwich.

"It's a community that is growing for Daddies and Littles to live without judgment or worry about the public. Here a Little girl like you can behave just as she wants to, and a Daddy can make sure that she's always safe and protected by others who know just how precious a Little is," he explained as her eyes widened.

"Only Daddies and Little girls live here?" Rita asked in amazement.

"Currently, only Daddies and Little girls are here full time, but Little boys are welcome here as well. Hunter and his Daddy come to visit often but their jobs keep them in town. I'm sure that Mommies would be invited to move in if someone vouched for them. The original investors in this big bundle of land were all men, but all are welcome here. As long as they understand our way of life," he explained to the beautiful woman who meant so much to him so quickly.

Silence descended over the kitchen as they both ate their sandwiches. When Rita finished her first half, Bart placed another on the tray. "Eat up, Ritagirl."

She tried to eat daintily, but she was so hungry. That first half disappeared like magic. Rita didn't want Bart to think she was a pig that overate. So, she tried to force herself to eat slowly. Chewing each bite fifty times and setting the sandwich down between each bite, Rita tried to use all those tricks that were supposed to help you cut down on the amount you wanted to eat.

When she next set the last bit of her meal down, Bart's hand covered hers. When Rita's eyes rose to meet his, she saw sincere concern written over his face. "What's wrong?" she asked.

"Are you feeling okay, honey? You're moving so jerkily. Is your head hurting?" he worried.

"Yeah, my head hurts, but not any more than ten minutes ago," she reassured him quickly. Then realizing that he had been watching her attempts not to overeat, her face blushed bright red, and her eyes dropped back to the tray. "I'm sorry. I'm so hungry. I don't want you to think I'm hogging the sandwiches," she admitted in a low whisper, too embarrassed to look at him.

"Ritagirl, look at me," Bart demanded as he squeezed the hand under his. When she didn't raise her eyes, his tone became more dominant, "Little girl, you may not have decided if I get to be your Daddy, but I have already made up my mind. You are mine. Look at me now!"

The sheer power of his tone drew her eyes to his. He hadn't raised his voice or hurt her hand. There was nothing that Rita could do but follow his directions. "I'm sorry," she repeated.

"I don't know what ass said something to you about eating too much. While I'm taking care of you, you will eat until you're no longer hungry. We will eat healthy most of the time because I want both of us to feel good. But we'll also have a treat now and then." He reached over and picked up another half to put on her tray. Then thinking better of it, he picked up two full sandwiches and put those on her tray. "Eat, Ritagirl."

"I can't eat that much!" she protested with a laugh.

"Eat what you like. I hope you'll learn that I am not that type of idiot who'd criticize or judge you for your eating habits." When she nodded her head no to deny that she thought badly of him, Bart said, "You are perfect. If you weighed twenty pounds less or fifty pounds more, I wouldn't think anything other than you are a perfect Little."

She searched his face looking for any sign that he wasn't completely honest. There wasn't any. *He really doesn't care,* she thought. The corners of her mouth tilted up as she looked at the handsome man next to her.

"Now, eat and drink your milk. I want you strong and healthy, so I can show you just how much I appreciate all your curves," Bart ordered as he picked up his milk glass and held it out to her.

Immediately, she plucked her drink from the tray and clinked her cup with his as if it was fine wine. Taking a big drink, Rita's face screwed up into a funny expression. It had been a long time since she drank milk.

"You'll get used to it, Ritagirl," Bart assured her as he gulped the cold liquid in his glass.

CHAPTER 10

R ita hadn't eaten two more sandwiches, but she had eaten
another half. Her stomach pooched slightly out as she watched
Bart lean over to turn on the faucet in the large soaking tub. She'd
wanted one of those for years. The idea of reading in the tub and not
having her feet, knees, or chest sticking out of the warm water
sounded heavenly. Now, the tub made her face turn red with
nervousness.

You have to take your clothes off to take a bath. The words echoed in
her mind, making her head hurt a bit worse. She swayed dizzily, and
Bart's hands wrapped around her waist to hold her steady.

"I've allowed you to do too much, Ritagirl. Your Daddy needs to
learn that you'll need lots of rest until you've recovered. I know you're
worried about being naked in front of me. I will try to be very clinical,
but my body's already betraying me," he said, shifting one hand to the
fly of his jeans as he adjusted himself.

He was hard. No, more than just hard, his shaft pressed urgently
against the heavy denim. The tip seemed barely contained by his
waistband. Shocked, her eyes jumped to his, and she swayed a
bit more as she paid the price for her darting gaze.

"Let me help you, Little girl," he murmured as he supported her
with one arm while pulling her t-shirt over her head with the other.

45

Exhausted, Rita knew that she couldn't do this by herself. His body had proven to her that her extra pounds didn't repel him. She leaned a shoulder against him for support, allowing him to unfasten her jeans and push them over her hips. In just a few minutes, Rita rested her head against the high porcelain tub as she soaked in the warm water.

She could hear Bart walking around the room before settling next to the tub. Keeping her eyes closed, Rita hoped the medicine that Bart had given her after eating would start working soon. She'd swallowed the two pain relievers to calm her headache. Bart had kissed her forehead when she'd thanked him for caring for her.

Now, she could feel him wipe a washcloth over her face washing the last lingering traces of the makeup that she'd put on so long ago. An image of looking in the mirror at herself while she applied makeup flashed into her brain, but she didn't get any details that would help her solve the mystery of who she was. She could just remember thinking that she needed to buy a new mascara. Sighing, she quieted her mind from thinking so hard. It just hurt.

"You won't be able to force your memory to come back, Ritagirl," Bart remarked in a hushed tone as he started to wash her shoulders before instructing. "Sit up for a minute and let me wash your back."

"I know. Sometimes, something is just hovering there," she complained as she leaned forward. The feel of the washcloth in his hand stroking over her skin brought a slight smile to her lips. No one had pampered her like this since her childhood. "Do all Daddies give their Little girls a bath?" she asked curiously as he rinsed her skin.

"Lie back, honey," came the next instruction as he helped her stretch out again against the slanted tub wall behind her. "I can't imagine why a Daddy wouldn't help his Little get clean," Bart remarked in a low, gruff voice that revealed his desire as he began to wash her torso.

Rita sucked in a deep breath as the washcloth glided over the side of one full breast. Both nipples had contracted when this man had undressed her. Now, they clenched into tighter buds. Her eyes peeked open to watch as Bart washed her skin. His thumb brushed over one sensitive peak, drawing a gasp from her lips.

"Such a pretty baby," Bart crooned as his hand cupped her breast for just a few seconds.

"Bart?" she whispered.

"I know, Ritagirl. My touch feels right to you, doesn't it?" His blue eyes captured her now fully open eyes as his touch moved to caress her other breast. When she nodded, he continued, "It's not time to play tonight, but soon."

She blushed furiously as that soft cloth in his talented fingers washed her entire body. Bart was very thorough washing from her head to her toes, making sure that every nook and cranny was clean. He didn't hesitate again, even when her breath caught in her chest as he spread her buttocks and labia to wash her most intimate areas.

Could this headache just go away? Rita fervently wished as her body instantly reacted to his touch. She knew, however, that Bart wouldn't reverse his decision. He would wait until she felt better to explore her body passionately.

After he helped her from the tub, Bart dressed her in an oversized t-shirt before tucking Rita into his bed. "I want to keep an eye on you throughout the night, Ritagirl. You'll sleep with me, okay?" he asked, pulling the soft bedding up to tuck under her chin.

Cuddled in warmth and softness, Rita's blinking eyes drifted shut without an answer. Almost instantly, she crashed into sleep, unaware of Bart's movements around the large master suite. When he slid under the covers to join her, her body unconsciously shifted against his freshly showered body.

"Goodnight, Ritagirl. I'm so glad I found you. I don't plan to let you go," he whispered to her before kissing the top of her head nestled in the curve of his shoulder.

"Okay, Daddy," she answered without waking up completely. "No squeezing," she admonished in the same whispering voice when Bart's arm tightened around her. His soft chuckles rocked her back into a deep sleep.

CHAPTER 11

Buzz, Buzz! Grumpy as the insistent sound interrupted her sleep, Rita hugged the heat source that she had wrapped herself around. When the hard surface under her cheek bounced slightly, she raised her head and sleepily looked into laughing blue eyes. "It's early," she informed him and lowered her head back to his shoulder.

"I have to get that, Ritagirl," he laughed as he reached for the buzzing phone on the nightstand. His arm steadied her when she clung to his body as he rolled slightly to grab the phone.

"Hello? Hi, Tyler!" Bart listened as the other man spoke.

Rita could hear the murmur of a low voice on the other end of the connection. She tried to wake up to listen to the conversation but decided it wasn't worth it, and her eyes drifted closed again. Listening to the rumble of Bart's voice and his steady heartbeat, Rita was almost back to sleep when Bart began easing her over to the side to free himself.

"Nooo," she protested, clinging to his body.

"There's a cow having trouble calving, Ritagirl. I need to go help. Go back to sleep. I'll be back as quick as possible," Bart explained as he firmly disengaged himself from her.

"Calving. That's having a baby, isn't it?" she asked between yawns.

"Yes. Sometimes nature needs some help. Close your eyes, Little girl. Dream pleasant dreams," he said as he stood and walked to the dresser. He turned on a small lamp sitting on the wooden top to be able to see.

In the pool of light, Rita's eyes widened at the sight of his broad shoulders and firm, nude butt. She had been lying against his skin but had been too tired to realize that he was completely naked. Her eyes closed to slits trying to pretend that she was asleep and not ogling his body as he turned to the side to begin opening drawers.

Her eyes blinked back open at the sight of his profile. Bart didn't have the bulging muscles of someone who lifted weights in a gym. She knew that he was strong. He'd carried her without strain several times. It flashed into her mind that his work with animals must have honed his body into this perfect shape.

Allowing her gaze to lower from his chest over his trim stomach, Rita must have made a small sound. Bart turned with briefs in his hand. In the dim light of the bedroom, he provided her with a perfect view of his penis. Thick and long, his manhood at rest made her push up from the bed onto one elbow.

A slow smile spread across Bart's mouth as he traced the path of her vision. "Little girl, your eyes are going to pop out," he teased as he stepped into the tight boxer briefs covering his nudity. He strode forward to the edge of the bed and leaned over, bringing their heads together. "If you're a good Little girl, Daddy will let you…"

The buzzing of the phone interrupted his next words. Dragging himself away, Bart grabbed the phone and answered it. "That's not good," he commented as he jogged to the closet and pulled out a faded pair of jeans and a t-shirt. Holding the phone between his shoulder and ear, he quickly dressed.

On his way out of the room, Bart paused in the doorway and covered the phone with his hand. "Go back to sleep. I'll be back as soon as possible. There's an emergency with a laboring cow. Wait here for me if you wake up, and I'm still gone. Understand? No disappearing!" he stressed before racing down the hall.

With the clunk of the door behind him and the sound of the

truck's engine, Rita knew that something urgent was happening. Moving to lie in the spot that Bart had been sleeping, she rested her head on his pillow and inhaled slowly. It smelled just like him. Sure that she wasn't sleepy, she closed her eyes so she could truthfully tell him she had tried to go to sleep.

CHAPTER 12

The smell of coffee woke her. Blinking into the sunshine filling the bedroom, Rita pushed herself up to sit on the comfortable mattress. "Bart?" she called.

"Yes, Little girl. It's me. I'm making breakfast for you. Just stay in bed, I'll bring it to you on a tray." Bart's low, masculine voice reassured her and made her smile.

"Breakfast in bed," she said out loud in the empty room. Pushing herself out from under the covers, Rita padded into the bathroom and used the toilet. She washed her face and hands before returning to the bedroom at the same time a barefoot Bart carried a laden, wooden tray into the room.

"You were supposed to stay in bed, Ritagirl," he reproached as he set down the tray on the padded bench at the end of the bed.

"I had to go to the bathroom," she explained as she climbed back into bed. "You changed clothes, and your hair is wet," she remarked, tilting her head to the side in confusion.

"Being a vet can be messy, honey. I have a shower stall and several changes of clothing in the laundry just off the entryway," he said with a smile as he covered her legs with the soft bedding before picking up the tray and returning to sit against the pillows and headboard. "Let's eat. I'm starving. I bet you are, too."

"Is the cow okay?" she asked, searching his face.

"No, Ritagirl. The cow was just too small for her big calf. It happens sometimes. Nature isn't always perfect. Between Tyler and I, we were able to save the calf. He's a whopper. We rounded up another cow with a new calf. She's accepted Goliath. He's nursing happily now," Bart reassured her.

"Can I see him?" she eagerly asked, ignoring the delicious smelling food on the tray.

"After breakfast, if your head is up to it, maybe," the tired vet hedged his answer. Bart scooped up some fluffy, scrambled eggs on the fork.

"My head feels better. Look, I can do this," Rita said, turning her head quickly to look in all the corners. "Whoa!" she muttered as her hand closed over Bart's thigh for stability as she became dizzy.

"You need to let your brain rest, Little girl. Sloshing it from one side to the other won't help you heal," Bart warned with a stern look. "Open up. Let's give your body some nutrition to fuel your recovery." When she followed his directions, Bart placed the food into her mouth.

"Mmmm! That's really good." Looking over the immense assortment of items on the tray, she leaned forward to sniff appreciatively. "Can I have some bacon? I love bacon!"

"Of course," After handing her a perfectly crisp piece of bacon, Bart fed himself a bite of eggs.

Companionably, they ate their breakfast together. Each time that Rita tried to eat something by herself, Bart stopped her and fed her. Soon, Rita stopped trying to help and just enjoyed being spoiled. When the pile of food was half-eaten, Rita couldn't take another bite.

"I'm so full. No more for me," she held her hand up to ward off the next bite that Bart lifted to her lips. She watched Bart inhale the remaining food on the tray and wondered how he could eat so much and stay in such fantastic shape. Mentally shaking her head at the injustice of how bodies, especially males versus females, processed calories.

"Would you like to go to the barn to see the calf?" Bart asked as he pushed the almost empty tray away.

"Don't you need to go back to sleep?" she asked in amazement.

"I'll take a nap with you later," he answered with a devastating grin.

"I don't usually take naps," she quickly answered.

"You do now. Give me five minutes to clean the kitchen and fill the dishwasher." Bart rolled out of bed with the ease of someone in great shape. He held a hand out to help Rita scramble out of bed. His eyes twinkled in amusement when she quickly tugged her borrowed t-shirt as far as possible down her thighs.

"Ritagirl, you'll get used to me seeing your body. I enjoy looking at my sweet Little girl," he reassured her.

"I'm kind of out of shape," she began trying to explain her extra weight.

"You are perfect, just as you are. I want you to start challenging that negative voice in your head that must be repeating that you're too heavy. It's important to feel good and be healthy. The size of the jeans you wear isn't." Bart gently lifted her chin up, so their eyes met. "I will never lie to you, Ritagirl. When I say that I love your body, I am telling you the truth. Okay?"

"O… okay," she whispered in a voice that quivered with uncertainty.

"Thank you. Now, let me get this tray. You lead the way. Do you remember how to get to the nursery?" Bart asked, ushering Rita into the hall before him.

Rita hesitated in the doorway. Moving her head carefully, she looked each way down the hallway. To the left, she could see a lighted room. *That must be the kitchen,* she thought. Pointing right, she looked over her shoulder at Bart for confirmation, "That way?"

"Exactly! The nursery is just across the hallway to the right," Bart confirmed. "Let's go turn the lights on so you can explore."

Walking into the dimly lit nursery, Rita was relieved to see that he'd turned a nightlight on for her. She never had liked the dark. "Oh, a hallway light shining into a bedroom just jumped into my mind," she rushed to share, hesitating in the doorway.

Bart turned on the lights and rubbed her shoulder. "Can you remember any details?" he probed.

Rita tried to pull anything else into her brain, but it was as if she'd run into a brick wall in her mind. "I know it was my apartment, but there's nothing else there. I keep getting flashes of my life. It's so frustrating," she told him, rubbing between her eyebrows to staunch the growing headache that always accompanied her efforts to remember anything.

"Give it time. Don't push. Go play, Ritagirl. I'll be back in a few minutes, and we'll get dressed to go to the barn," Bart urged. He stepped around her and opened the thick window shades allowing the morning light to shine inside before dropping a kiss on the top of her head and leaving the nursery.

Standing in the doorway, Rita peered into the nursery before taking a few steps inside. She knew that she'd already slept in her crib, but that had been without her knowledge. Now, she knew it was a nursery. That changed everything.

She walked to the crib and turned to lean against it as she looked around the beautiful room. Rita loved the color of the walls. They were the same color as the lightest lilacs that had filled her grandmother's garden. She'd always wanted purple walls, but living in an apartment meant you had to get permission to paint anything. The mere mention that she wanted to use purple received an instant refusal from the landlord. She'd had to settle for purple curtains instead.

Wrapping her arms around her shoulders, Rita hugged herself to celebrate just a few more bits of knowledge about her old life coming back into her mind. Feeling a little less lost, she walked over to the closet and opened the door. Mostly empty, two outfits were hanging inside. Rita dismissed the possibility that both the cute dress and the colorful t-shirt and leggings would fit with a quick glance. Her bottom lip stuck out a little as she worried that Bart really did care about her size and that he wouldn't want to be her Daddy if someone more petite came along.

As she closed the door and wandered to the curiously padded table that she had wondered about earlier. With each step, her eyes noticed something new. There were a bunch of folded white padded things with colorful designs. Plucking one off the top of one stack, she unfolded it. *A diaper!* The words ricocheted through her head.

In some of the books she'd read, the Mommies and Daddies had dressed their Littles in a diaper. Some didn't have to use it, but many were required to potty into it. Her heart raced a bit at the idea. *Would Bart wish to take such intimate care of her?* she wondered. The thought both thrilled and petrified her.

Quickly refolding and piling it back with the others, Rita turned her back on what was obviously a changing table. She walked to the big chest and scooped up the stuffed zebra that sat on top, grinning at her. Petting the soft fur, she hugged the toy to her chest and squeezed him.

"You're so soft," she complimented the stuffie. "Do you belong to anyone? I'd love to have a stuffie like you. Would you mind hanging out with me for a while? You know until you see if someone better comes along?" she asked in a quiet troubled voice. The small clothes in the closet weighed heavily on her mind. That diaper had looked too small to fit around her, as well.

Sliding down to the floor, Rita dropped her forehead against the comforting zebra's mane. Had there ever been anyone who had wanted her just as she was? She wasn't wearing a wedding ring, so she didn't think that she was married. She'd know if she was married, right? Her mind whirled a million miles a minute. Somehow, she knew inside that she hadn't ever walked down the aisle to marry anyone.

A large body settled onto the carpet next to her and pulled her sideways into his lap. "Ritagirl, you're going to give yourself a headache. What are you thinking so hard about?"

"You don't want a heavy Little," burst from her mouth before she could stop it. Rita leaned away from his body to see his face.

"Wow! You're really worried about that. What put that thought back into your mind?" He asked, rubbing her back with one hand. Her eyes betrayed her and strayed over to the partially cracked closet door.

"Oh, I see. You found the clothes that Jeremy and Beau hid over here at my house, so Shelby wouldn't find them. They are taking their Little girl to the big city to see a musical and wanted to surprise her. Shelby is very observant. They knew that if she noticed some of her clothing missing that she would start asking questions. So they bought a dress for her to wear to the performance and a set of comfortable clothes to wear home," he explained easily as he watched her face.

"Really?" He hadn't seemed to make up an answer, but could the clothing really be just someone else's?

"Really. Now, if you looked in the drawers over there," he pointed to a tall chest, "you would have found a few outfits in different sizes. Moving to SANCTUM has been magic for some of the men who are building here. Their Little has just appeared out of empty air. We've learned that it's a good idea to have several sizes available so that we can clothe whoever shows up next. I have a couple of medium sizes of t-shirts and a couple of x-larges. I bought stretchy leggings that will fit a variety of Little girls."

"Really?" she repeated, searching his face to make sure he wasn't deceiving her.

Bart laughed when she repeated the same question. After pulling Rita and her new stuffed friend in for a quick hug, he leaned back with a smile. "You can ask me over and over. It's okay. I will always give you the same answer. I've been looking for my Little girl for a long time. I'm sure you're her." Cupping her jaw with his hand, he leaned in to kiss her lips deeply.

When they were both breathing heavily, he leaned back again with a pleased smile. "No one but my Little girl would taste as good as you do, Rita." Sobering, he told her, "I'm going to take very good care of you while we're figuring out who you are and what was happening the night we met. But remember this. You are mine."

Rita nodded happily. Plucking the stuffie from the floor where it had flopped while she enjoyed Bart's kisses, she squeezed the soft zebra to her chest. Suddenly, this room felt like home.

CHAPTER 13

T hat friendly zebra covered her eyes a few minutes later. Bart had lifted her onto the changing table. He stretched a thick strap across her chest, tethering her in place. Automatically, she tested it, trying to sit up. Her body responded, and she clenched her thighs together to hide the gush of arousal as she learned restraint turned her on completely.

Bart didn't comment on her actions but simply continued his preparations. He pulled her nightshirt up to her waist. Holding her ankles, he lifted her legs straight up and then pulled them back toward her face, raising and spreading her bottom.

Rita could feel the air on her most private places. Struggling automatically, she discovered that this position and the thick strap controlled her movements. He was entirely in charge. She froze as Bart pressed a lubricated finger against her tight anus. "What? Stop Bart!" she demanded as she tried to wiggle away.

His finger continued to slide slowly into her narrow passage despite her efforts to resist. "Little girl, you are not in charge here. I need to make sure you are healing and don't need to return to the hospital. Littles have their temperatures taken in their bottoms. It is more accurate. Relax. I will not hurt you," he promised.

Penetrated fully by one thick finger, Rita finally relaxed her muscles. Only then did he withdraw the lubricating digit and slide a thick thermometer deep into her rectum. She shivered slightly at the feel of the cold invader. "I don't like this," she wailed to Bart.

"Temperature time will soon become normal for you," he assured Rita. "Just relax and let your Daddy take care of you."

"All Daddies do this?" she questioned, sure that this was not normal.

"All Mommies and Daddies know that many things can influence an oral temperature. Like the cold milk, you just drank at breakfast. It automatically dropped your temperature. All Mommies and Daddies who care deeply about their Littles take their temperature rectally," he explained without hesitation or any sign that this was not the norm.

"Can't you take it out now? I feel fine!" she rushed to assure him.

"Daddy is in charge. Let's see if I can help you relax." Bart placed a weighted fabric block against the end of the thermometer, snuggled next to her buttocks to hold it fully implanted with the oversized end securing the instrument safely outside. Switching the hand that held her ankles pinned forward, the handsome man traced her outer labia forward between her thighs. Another gush of slick fluid allowed him to glide his fingers through her hidden pink folds to trace her other opening.

Embarrassed to have him discover how wet she had become, Rita struggled to move again. This time, each movement jarred the thermometer inside her body. Rita's eyes flashed to meet his. "No, Bart. Don't ..." she began to protest automatically, but her voice trailed away as his fingers began to stroke her automatically.

Sure that she should not be enjoying this, she rocked slightly in an attempt to move away from the pleasure but only increased it as the intruder in her bottom pressed deep inside her body. Instantly, Rita moved toward those tantalizing fingers. Unable to stop herself from repeating this slight movement over and over, her eyes peeked up at Bart to check his expression. Was she disgusting him?

As her brown eyes met his blue ones, Bart's hoarse voice revealed the extent that he enjoyed bringing her pleasure, "Daddies always take care of their Littles. Let me help you, Ritagirl."

"Please," she begged as her excitement continued to grow. Her eyes drifted shut as she concentrated on the sensations between her legs. What had been a cold invader now seemed fiery hot. "Aaah!" she cried into the room as her body contracted into a body tingling orgasm.

His fingers slowed, pressing against her sensitive clitoris, extending the pleasure almost to the point of pain. When she could take no more, his fingers lifted from her body. She missed his touch instantly as her body melted onto the padded top.

Bart removed the thermometer and the soft, weighted cube. Without a moment's hesitation, he leaned down to pick out a diaper from the stacks below. Lifting her ankles once again, Bart slid the padding under her hips before releasing her ankles and guiding them set widely apart to the padded surface. After expertly securing the diaper in place, Bart dressed his Little in a comfortable outfit before helping her slide to the ground.

"You want me to wear a diaper?" she shakily asked, patting her hip.

"We'll decide whether you always wear diapers or not when we know more about your Little. For today, you're soaking wet. A diaper will make you feel more comfortable. Right?" he asked, watching her digest all the information he had included in the conversation.

Her face mirrored the wheels that whirled in her mind, and she processed all that had happened. Finally, she changed the conversation to give herself more time to think. "I need to wear a bra. I can't go out anywhere or see anyone like this?" she worried. Her hand brushed the front of the t-shirt she wore. Her still erect nipples pointed through the soft cotton.

"No one will stare. I promise you. They'll appreciate a beautiful Little, but they would never make you feel uncomfortable," he reassured her with a smile. "We'll get some supportive undershirts to make you feel more comfortable. For today, will you try wearing what you have on now?"

Looking skeptically at him, she finally nodded slowly. The first person who laughed at the fat woman in a diaper and no bra was going to get it. Rita leaned over to pick up the zebra she had dropped as Bart pleasured her. She'd just hold it in front of her to hide.

CHAPTER 14

Wearing a pair of those soft, stretchy leggings and a beautiful jade-colored t-shirt that matched them perfectly, Rita squealed as Bart lifted her into the truck. It was a short walk to the barn, but Bart didn't want Rita to exert herself for several days to allow her brain to rest. It was easier to drive to see the new calf.

The door was open when they got there. Bart helped Rita from the truck and took her hand to lead her inside. Rita missed the large, stuffed zebra that Bart had convinced her to leave at home, so it didn't get dirty in the barn. One person was already at the railing of the enclosure. A young woman turned as they walked in.

"Come see!" a slender brunette invited before turning back to look at the calves. "They're so cute!" She didn't react to Rita's physical appearance in any way. The young woman just welcomed her like they were fast friends.

Rita hung back as Bart led her to the fence. She didn't know why she felt shy. It was different to relax and let her Little side out when they were alone. She guessed she was afraid to have others make fun of her.

When Rita was just a few steps away, the brunette turned and walked forward to hug her. The stranger heeded Bart's quick warning to be careful with Rita, and her arms were gentle and loving as they wrapped around her.

Leaning back, the smiling brunette whispered, "I'm sorry you've been hurt. I'm Priscilla. You're safe here."

"I'm Rita," she answered, unable to resist the friendliness of the other woman.

"Hi, Rita. Come see the newest calf and his new sister," Priscilla invited, stepping back to take Rita's hand and pull her gently to the railings. "Isn't he cute? Daddy went to get some milk for us to feed them. I can't wait."

Looking at the spindly legs holding up the wobbly calf, Rita had to smile. He was simply adorable. Each time his adoptive mom licked his head, the calf teetered on the brink of falling over. But he was stubborn and stood his ground.

Any self-conscious thought in her mind melted away as her heart melted for the cute baby animal. Bart was right. They didn't care about silly things. Besides, bras were really uncomfortable sometimes.

A tall, dark-haired man joined the group. He was carrying two large bottles filled with a milky substance. "Sugar, you have a new friend," he said, warmly as Priscilla ran to meet him with a hug.

"This is Rita. We have to be careful with her. She's been hurt," Priscilla shared before excitedly rushing on. "Can we feed the calves, Daddy?"

Mitch's eyes met Bart's over the women's heads. At the latter's nod, he knew all the information he needed. "Hi, Rita. I'm sorry you're injured. I think you'll find SANCTUM is the best place to heal. Would you like to feed the calves with my Little girl, Priscilla?"

Rita's eyes flew back and forth between Priscilla and Mitch. They were so upfront about their relationship. Quickly, she covered her reaction by slowly nodding her sensitive head. "I'd love to feed one."

Neither Little girl had ever bottle-fed a calf, so Mitch and Bart helped their Littles hold the bottle at first. Both calves were hungry and enthusiastically pulled on the large nipple topping each bottle. Delighted giggles filled the air as both Priscilla and Rita enjoyed the young animals' antics.

When each bottle was emptied, the calves played for a short time before curling up in the straw together for a nap. It was evident that the adopted calf had been fully incorporated into the small family. After giving the mama cow a few sweet oats to fuel her milk production, Bart shooed everyone away.

"Time to leave, everyone. Let's give the new family some time to rest. Everyone's going to need to replenish their energy," he said as he ushered them through the barn door.

Rita slipped her hand into his when they stopped outside the large structure. She looked curiously at the new people as the men talked about the calving taking place on the SANCTUM grounds. Taking a step forward, she bravely decided to ask some questions.

Smiling at the friendly brunette, she said, "Hi, Priscilla. Have you lived here long?"

"I've been here for a few months. It's the best place. You will love it here," Priscilla enthused. "Are you Little like us?" the brunette openly asked.

Rita looked back at Bart. He was still talking, but she knew he was listening. Turning back to look at Priscilla, she answered, "I think I've always dreamed of being a Little girl." Despite all the holes scattered through her memories, Rita remembered learning about Littles and knowing that she was one.

"You think you've dreamed of being Little?" Priscilla asked in confusion.

Automatically, Rita's hand went to the knot on her head. "I hit my head, and I don't remember a lot of stuff," she shared.

"There's a lot of stuff that I'd like to forget," Priscilla laughed before sobering to add, "That has to be scary. I'm sorry to joke."

"That's okay. I'm sorry that you've got bad stuff to forget." Impulsively, Rita stepped forward to hug Priscilla, who squeezed her back tightly.

When she stepped away, Priscilla took her hand and turned to the men. "Daddy, can Rita come over to play? I'd like to get to know her better."

Mitch warmly answered, "Of course, she can if it's okay with her Daddy."

Rita looked at Bart with a hopeful smile. "Can I, Daddy?" The word, Daddy, just came automatically. She knew it was important, and she didn't use it lightly. Just as Bart seemed to know that she was his, Rita loved how he had taken care of her since they'd met. While most of her memories were gone, her injury truly hadn't erased her inner nature. She was a Little.

His eyes grew warmer as he allowed her to see the passion that he felt toward her. Her acknowledgment he was her Daddy for the first time burned deep into his heart. For a few seconds, it was as if they were the only people in SANCTUM. "I will bring Rita over in a couple of hours to play. She needs to take a nap now," he said without taking his gaze away from her.

"That's great. Come over whenever it's convenient. Come on, Priscilla. Let's see who can walk home the fastest," Mitch said to distract his Little girl.

"Why does she have to take a nap now, Daddy? Didn't she just get out of bed?" Priscilla's voice drifted back to Rita and Bart as they hustled away. Mitch's hushed masculine voice couldn't be understood, but there was no disguising Priscilla's reaction.

"Oh! That's why they're going back to bed." The footsteps kept receding. Then the last thing they heard was, "I've been really good, Daddy."

"Good Littles deserve a reward, don't they, Ritagirl?" Bart asked with a slow, heated smile.

"I've been really good, Daddy," Rita parroted Priscilla's words.

"Let's get in the truck, honey. I need to get you home."

CHAPTER 15

Bart drove home quickly but smoothly to prevent jarring his Little girl. As he drove with her buckled into the middle part of the bench seat, Bart considered how to make love to her without worsening the effects of her concussion. His eyes glanced over to mesh with hers often. *She's mine.*

Putting the truck into park in the large garage, Bart turned to wrap his hand around the back of her neck and pull Rita in for a kiss. Lifting his head, Bart warned, "Stay in your seat. I will come to get you." When she nodded, Bart let himself out of the truck cab and jogged around to open her door.

"Wha… aat?" she gasped as he lifted her from the truck and began to carry her across the garage toward the door. "I'm too heavy," she protested only to close her mouth with a snap as he met her eyes with a very disapproving look. Rita decided that she should trust him to know his own strength. She simply pushed open the door between the garage and the kitchen as he paused at the door.

"Good girl," he praised her, dropping a kiss to the top of her head.

Extraordinarily pleased by his simple praise, Rita pressed a kiss to the suntanned skin at the base of his throat. She clung to his shoulders in surprise when he lowered her to sit on the kitchen table. "I'm not hungry," she rushed to assure him, afraid that he had decided to feed her rather than fulfill the promise of his earlier passionate looks.

"I'm suddenly starving," he answered, stepping between her knees, forcing her thighs to spread widely apart. His fingers hooked under the hem at the bottom of her t-shirt and began to lift.

Rita raised her arms to allow him to pull off her shirt, revealing her full breasts. Automatically in the bright light of the kitchen, her arms started to cover her chest.

"Little girl, do not hide your body from your Daddy," he commanded with a tone that made her freeze in place before she forced her hands back to her lap. "Good, Ritagirl."

His passion-filled blue eyes held hers until she whispered, "Okay, Daddy!" The slow smile that answered her agreement made her sit taller, inviting his perusal. Only then did his eyes caress over the soft skin he'd revealed. The path of his gaze heating her body without a single touch of his fingers.

"Such a beautiful Little," he complimented as he leaned forward to kiss her. As his lips softly wooed her, one large hand cupped the back of her head. When he had her held securely in place, his lips became more demanding as he swept his tongue into her mouth to taste her sweetness, drawing moans of delight from their throats. Slowly, he leaned forward, pressing her back against the smooth, cool oak table. His cupping hand protecting her head from any sudden movement or impact.

Rita's fingers clutched his shirt, holding him close when he lifted his lips. Panting slightly from the hot kisses, she wiggled under him, enjoying the feel of his shirt against her bare skin. There was something totally hot about being topless under the press of his fully clothed body. She clung to him as he began to shift backward as his lips kissed the tender skin under her jawline and down the delicate curve of her neck.

His fingers gripped the sides of her waist before sliding over her ribs to brush the sides of her breasts. She shivered under his light touch, hoping that his fingers would move to cup her breasts. When he didn't but just continued to tease her, Rita begged, "Please, Daddy. Touch me!"

Whispering against her skin, Bart asked, "Where, honey? Here?" His hands slid across her skin to cover each breast, trapping her nipples between two long fingers. He compressed those tight buds until she moaned in reaction and arched her chest up toward him.

When he straightened away from her body, she reached out, trying to hold him to her. "Shhh! Little girl, I'm going to protect your head. I'm not leaving," he promised. Bart reached one hand over his head and grabbed the back of his shirt in one large fist. Pulling upward, he stripped his shirt off and leaned back forward. He lifted her head gently and cushioned her skull with the soft cotton of the discarded garment.

"You need to lie still, Ritagirl. I don't want you to jostle your head. Will you do that for me?" he asked.

"I'll try," she whispered.

"Good, girl," he praised and rewarded her with a kiss that swept her breath away before lifting his lips and rewarding her with a line of kisses trailing to one impudent nipple.

She felt the heat of his breath as he hovered over the tight bud. Urgently, she begged, "Please. Please, Daddy. Make love to me!"

His lips instantly closed around her nipple and pulled it into his warm mouth. His tongue flicked back and forth over the tip, evoking a moan of pleasure from her. Afraid that he would stop again if she moved, Rita tried to stay still. Her fingers sunk into Bart's thick hair as she urged him for more.

Jumping slightly as the fingers, on one hand, tweaked her other nipple, Rita froze underneath him as pleasure zinged through her breast. As his hand moved to cup her fullness and lift that sweet mound toward him, his mouth released one tip and moved to lavish kisses on the other. Her eyes closed as she concentrated on the sensations that were building in her body.

When his hand slide over her plump stomach to push down the leggings, Rita peeked up at him. Afraid that he would dislike her rounded curves, she relaxed instantly. His face was a mask of male arousal that never wavered or changed. His appreciation of her body was carved into his expression.

Thrusting old insecurities out of her mind, Rita bent her knees to place her feet against the edge of the table. She lifted her hips to help him as he tugged the leggings off. Bart quickly pulled the oversized boots that he had loaned her to wear to the barn and tossed those to the side before unfastening her unused diaper and tossing it into the garbage.

She lie nude on the cool table as he stepped back slightly from the edge of the table. His eyes devoured the display of her most private area. With a groan, he stroked hard down the front of his bulging jeans. "Ritagirl, I want you to be sure. Are you ready for this big step?" he questioned, watching her face for any sign of indecision or discomfort.

Smiling at him, Rita felt more powerful than she ever had. She had caused the erection that strained the denim. This handsome man wanted her as much as she wanted him. The earlier climax had been incredible, but she needed to feel him inside her—feel him possess her. Reaching out to him again, she repeated, "Please, Daddy!"

Rita's eyes stayed glued to his fingers as Bart slowly unbuttoned the fly of his jeans. After grabbing a small packet from his pocket and tossing it on the table next to her, he pushed them over the hard butt that she'd ogled each time she had followed him. As they dropped to the floor, his hands were already lifting the waistband of his boxer briefs over the erection that stretched the cotton fabric. When those also fell around his ankles, Bart stepped closer once again.

One hand cupped her cheek, and he leaned over her to kiss her fiercely. His free hand gently sliding under her head to cushion her skull from being pressed into the wood below her. Lifting his lips and body from her, those skillful hands stroked down the sides of her body. Stopping here and there to caress and tease, Bart seemed to know exactly where she needed to be touched and how.

He played her body like a beautiful cello. Stroking here and there, she soon forgot her promise to lie still. His hands pressed her to the table to restrain her movements and keep her safe. She loved the constraint as his muscular body controlled her movements. Her body hummed under this touch. Rita didn't think she'd ever been so turned on.

When his hands left her to open the condom packet, the crinkle made her wetter in anticipation. Avidly, she watched him roll the protection over his long, thick penis. Unconsciously licking her lips at the sight of his hand stroking his erection, Rita tried to scoot closer to him.

Once fully protected, he lifted her right foot from the edge of the table and drew it toward his body to hook her knee over his shoulder. Sliding his hands under her full hips, Bart lifted her slightly from the table and pulled her bottom over the edge. He closed the slight gap between their bodies immediately as he stepped forward to rub his shaft against the slick pink folds between her legs.

A low moan erupted from both of their mouths as their bodies pressed together. Watching between her separated thighs, Rita froze as Bart fit the wide head of his penis against her opening. His words sent a shiver of awareness through her body.

"Once I make you mine, I will never let you go," Bart warned. The strain of holding himself back, combined with passion, tightened the shoulder muscles under her knee.

"Make me yours, Daddy. I want to be with you," she rushed to say.

With a flex of his hips, the thick head of his penis began to move slowly into her body. Bart didn't rush. He allowed her body to contract and then relax as his body glided into her body on a sea of wetness. His gaze caressed her body as he held her left leg now wrapped around his back and the thigh of her right one that lay against his body.

When the tip of his erection reached the mouth of her womb, Bart reversed and began to pull slowly out. With rigid control etched in his face, the caring man maintained this gentle stroke in and out. His eyes devoured the view of her body displayed in front of him and the sight of his thick shaft gliding in and out of her body.

"Please," she begged as she writhed on the table. The sensations he drew from her body brought her quickly to the edge of something amazing. Rita bit her lip in anticipation as she strained toward the onslaught of pleasure that she could feel lurking just outside her reach.

She reached a hand to Bart in supplication. Gasping in surprise as he drew her hand between her thighs, her eyes met his in shock. Was he asking her to do what she thought?

"Touch yourself, Ritagirl. Your Daddy wants to know what brings you pleasure. Show me what you like," he demanded.

"But…" her voice trailed off in embarrassment.

"There are no lies between a Little girl and her Daddy, Ritagirl. Show Daddy how you pleasure yourself," he urged as his body continued its slow thrusts in and out. His fingers pressed hers into the wetness, and he began to move her fingers over her inner labia and clitoris.

Rita missed his slow smile when her eyes closed to concentrate on the sensations he was helping build between her legs. Her fingers began to move under his, showing him the rhythm and type of touch she enjoyed. To his delight, she even revealed her secret arousal points. When his hand lifted from hers, she continued unbidden.

Bart gripped her thigh, holding her close as his pelvis flexed to bring her pleasure. When her passion-glazed eyes met his, she knew that he would never let her go. She was his—the Little that he had dreamed of finding. Rita's lips parted to share a smile filled with promise and passion. He was hers as well.

CHAPTER 16

Both Littles giggled at the sight of the other's damp hair. The telltale sign of their afternoon showers following the passion that they had each shared with their Daddies. They shared a snack of cookies and milk on the small table in Priscilla's beautiful nursery. Overflowing with happiness, the two Littles chattered easily as they got to know each other.

"You don't remember anything?" Priscilla asked with wide eyes.

"I know my name is Rita. I remember a phone number, but it was disconnected. The police detective is trying to figure out who I am. I think Daddy, er, Bart is investigating too." Rita's face blushed red at her slip in not using Bart's name.

"It's safe here. You can call him Daddy if you wish," Priscilla shared, before taking another bite of the chocolate chip cookie. Her Daddy had helped her make them yesterday. She wasn't allowed to use the oven without his supervision. "I had always dreamed of finding a Daddy who would love me. All those books couldn't be wrong, right? Daddies had to exist."

Her jaw dropped open, and Rita stared at her. "You read books, too? My e-reader was packed with age play books."

"Me, too. It still is. Now, Daddy just reads them to me. Sometimes we act out the spicy parts. That's my favorite. Bringing the story alive, just as I imagined when I was alone in my room," Priscilla confessed before taking another bite.

That reminded Rita that she also held a cookie. Taking a bite, she chewed thoughtfully before sharing, "I had all sorts of books on my e-reader. I hope they didn't open my purse when they found it at the bar. I kept thinking I should put a password on my e-reader to make sure that no one could open it and read the titles of all the books in there. I never did because it's such a pain to enter it each time," Rita said blithely as she decided what spot to bite next to get the most chocolate chips.

The quiet that followed her statement, drew her attention to Priscilla, who looked at her in shock. "What?" Rita asked, self-consciously.

"You're remembering things. You left your purse in a bar. Maybe someone gave you a roofie?" Priscilla jumped up and whirled around.

Racing to her crib, she leaned over to talk into a purple stuffed hippopotamus' belly. "Daddy! Daddy, come quick! Rita remembers stuff!"

Rapid heavy footsteps in the hallway announced the men's progression before they burst into the room. "Rita? Are you okay, honey?" Bart asked in concern as he walked to her side quickly and dropped to sit on the floor next to her low chair.

"I'm okay," she reassured him.

"We were talking about age play books, and Rita mentioned that she hoped no one had opened her e-reader that she'd left in her purse when they find it at the bar," Priscilla rushed to fill in the concerned Daddies. She crawled onto Mitch's lap when he seated himself on the carpet following Bart's example. "Do you think someone put something in her drink?

"When Gumdrop found Rita, she didn't appear to be drugged. We were outside a pool hall. Do you think that's where you left your purse?" he questioned Rita gently.

Screwing up her nose as she tried to remember, Rita finally shook her head. "I don't think I was there for a drink. I remember the ingredients in drinks, like in a froufrou cosmopolitan. I can see my hands pouring alcohol into a shaker. I think I was a bartender," she announced triumphantly.

Bart kissed the side of her head and pulled out his phone. Finding the police officer's number, he pressed the button. Everyone in the nursery fell silent as they listened to the faint sound of the telephone connecting.

"This is Officer Doug Hamilton," the deep voice answered the phone.

"Officer Hamilton, this is Bart Jennings. We met when you came to interview a young woman who had lost her memory at the hospital. Rita is starting to remember a few things…" he started when the other man interrupted.

"Mr. Jennings, I can't reveal any information about the case without Rita's permission," the officer informed him. "Is she with you now?"

"Yes, she is here. Let me turn on the speakerphone." After a look at Rita to get her okay to share the information, Bart quickly pressed a button on the device to broadcast the conversation into the nursery. "Officer Hamilton, we can both hear you now."

"Hi, Officer," Rita said in a quiet voice to let him know that she was there and listening.

"Do I have your permission to speak freely in front of Mr. Jennings, Rita?"

"Yes, of course!" Rita rushed to assure him before blurting, "We think I worked in a bar."

"You did, indeed. The video surveillance of the poolhall revealed that you entered with Eddie Shaffer, the owner of The Country Tavern where you have bartended for slightly over two years. A couple of the waitresses called into the station to report that you disappeared without any of your belongings. I had already picked up Mr. Shaffer for questioning when I observed you entering the pool-hall with him on the security tapes for that night. You didn't appear to be there voluntarily," the officer began filling in the blanks in her memory.

"What's my name?" she implored him.

"Margarita Alma, you're thirty-two," he informed her.

Rita's mind raced in a million directions with all the information that began clicking into place. When Bart tugged her out of the chair to sit in his lap, she quickly shifted, thankful to have his arms around her. Things were starting to fall into place. It was almost more disturbing to have bits and pieces floating around her head than to have her mind be totally blank.

Bart asked the officer a few questions. Rita didn't absorb any of their conversation, and she tried to sort through the mess that her memories had become. Finally, she abruptly interrupted Bart to ask, "Am I a good person?"

The officer was very quiet for a couple of seconds. That was not a question that he had been expecting. "Rita, I can't make a judgment call like that. I've never met you before you lost your memory. I can tell you that your coworkers were very concerned about you. They all risked their jobs to call and report that you were missing. I've dealt with a lot of different types of people in this job. Very few people risk their own livelihood on someone who is a bad person."

Silence filled the air once again before the officer spoke again. "I have your purse. I'd like to interview you officially for the case that is mounting against your boss. Would you be able to come to talk to me?" Officer Hamilton asked. His tone had softened from the impersonal official approach that he had used when first speaking to her.

"We can be there tomorrow at eleven. Will that work for you?" Bart answered for her as he rocked her back and forth slightly.

"That will be fine. Keep a low profile. I didn't have all the facts I have now, and without your sworn statement that you remember what happened, I had to release him. Eddie Shaffer will be more dangerous now. Keep your eyes open. Would you like a police escort into town?" he asked.

"If we have any problems, we'll call you," Bart answered before disconnecting the call.

"Wow!" commented Priscilla wryly. "Those cookies are magic. You ate part of one and look at all we know now, Margarita."

"My grandmother is the only one who calls me, Margarita." Rita's offhand comment underlined the randomness of her returning memories, making them all smile.

"I'll just call you, Rita," Priscilla assured her.

CHAPTER 17

Rita clung to Bart's hand as he thanked Mitch and Priscilla for welcoming his Little. He knew that she considered him to be the one thing that she could rely upon as her mind began to remember everything. Boosting her back into the truck, Bart allowed her to think without interruption. He'd be there when she needed him.

Once back at his house, Bart helped her slide safely from the cab before leading her into the house. He sat her in a kitchen chair just long enough to make her a bottle before guiding her to the nursery. Sitting in the rocking chair, Bart pulled her onto his lap and pushed gently with his legs to sway back and forth. Rita curled against his chest to nestle her head under his chin.

Minutes passed. Bart could almost hear the gears in her head grinding together. His hand brushed over her head through her soft brown hair. He loved that she looked to him for security and protection when she was utterly befuddled. There wasn't anywhere else that he wished to be.

"I remember a lot, but there are bits here and there that I don't know. It's so frustrating," Rita finally shared.

"It will all come back. Try thinking about something else for a bit. Give your mind a rest," Bart suggested shifting her to lie back in the crook of his arm. He picked up the warm bottle of the milky formula and held it to her lips. "Drink, Ritagirl! Just relax and drink for Daddy."

To his delight, her eyes closed as she began to suck the delicious formula from the bottle. He rocked her slowly in the restful quiet of the nursery. By the time the bottle was almost empty, his Little was asleep. Suspecting that rest would enable her mind to sort itself out into a more comprehensible order, Bart relaxed and enjoyed holding her.

He would hate to admit that he was afraid that she wouldn't need him when all her memories returned. Trying to memorize her face, Bart allowed himself to study his sweet Ritagirl. *She's mine*, he decided. Bart knew that he would do anything possible to help her through whatever threat had spooked her into running away. He could only hope that she would want to stay with him when everything was settled.

CHAPTER 18

"He had drugs," Rita whispered an hour later.

Rousing from his thoughts, Bart's rough voice answered her, "Who?"

Those beautiful brown eyes opened to meet the blue eyes that captivated her. Her voice stayed soft. "Eddie Schaffer, the new owner of the bar. I walked in on him, snorting some powder. He made me leave with him. I didn't have a choice. He had a gun and threatened to shoot people in the bar."

"So, you put yourself in danger to save the others," Bart said, sadly shaking his head.

"I didn't have a choice," she admitted, searching his face to see if he was angry with her.

"I know, Ritagirl. I'm proud of you for thinking of others. I'd rather you watched out for yourself, but I have a feeling that you don't do that often," Bart said, running his hand through her silky hair.

Her eyes closed in appreciation of his caress. "I don't want to leave here," she confessed.

"I know, honey. But with someone like Eddie Shaffer, it's best to take him out of the equation quickly. He won't give up," the handsome man warned.

"I know." Rita curled up to sit up on his lap. "My head feels better now, but there are still a lot of things out of place. Can I tell you everything tomorrow?" she asked, staring into those blue eyes that looked at her like no man ever had.

"Yes," he answered as he leaned in to kiss her sweet lips. Chasing the flavor of the formula that clung to her lips, Bart explored her mouth, leaving them both breathing heavily.

As he sat back, she asked, "That's it? You don't have any questions?"

His slow smile brought an answering curve to her lips. "I'm your Daddy. I'll always have questions. You'll tell me when you can," he confidentially answered, stroking her arm with the side of his finger.

"Can we go see Gumdrop?"

Her question started him. His smile morphed into a grin of delight. "Gumdrop would love to see you, Ritagirl. Shall we go now?"

"I'd like that," the Little girl answered with twinkling eyes.

CHAPTER 19

Several horses turned to look curiously over their gates as the two entered the barn. Rita's eyes were glued to one stall. The gentle mare nickered happily at the sight of the Little girl who had treated her to sugar cubes. Sticking her head over the half gate, Gumdrop watched as Rita walked slowly to greet her as well. The Little girl had listened to her Daddy warn that she needed to move slowly, so she didn't spook the horse.

"Hi, Gumdrop!" Tentatively, Rita reached forward to stroke the mare's forehead. When Gumdrop whinnied and nosed back into Rita's caressing hand, making her giggle in delight. "You like me!" she said in amazement, looking back at Bart.

"Of course, she likes you. We need to give Gumdrop a little activity. I don't want you to ride her for a few days so we make sure we don't jostle your head, but we should take her to the corral for some exercise. Would you like to walk her around?" Bart asked as he plucked a bridle from the rack against the wall.

The vet knew that Gumdrop would be fine to wander around free by herself in the corral. He wanted Rita to feel needed and to strengthen the growing bond between the horse and the young women. Leading Gumdrop to the fenced-in area, he handed the bridle to Rita and urged her to walk slowly around. The Little began whispering to the horse on her second step. Gumdrop's ears perked up as the new mare listened carefully.

After watching several laps, Bart left the two alone to go muck out the stables. The men who stored horses in the barn took turns cleaning. He'd missed several rounds because of his work in the city, so Bart worked his way through all the stalls. Between each one, he stopped to check on his Little girl and Gumdrop.

As he cleaned, Bart checked on the horses and made a mental note of any concerns. It looked like they needed to have a farrier come take care of the horses' feet. Several needed some attention to their hooves and horseshoes. When finished, he washed his hands before pulling out his phone and sending a text. Luckily, there was a farrier in a nearby town that he trusted.

Removing his cowboy hat to wipe his brow, Bart exited the stable to see Rita perched on the top railing of the fence. Gumdrop stood in front of her with her graceful arched neck and head cocked slightly to the side as if she listened intently to whatever Rita was saying. He walked slowly to the corral, not wishing to startle either beautiful creature.

Gumdrop noticed him first. The mare bobbed her head in a greeting that caused Rita to turn around smiling. "Hi, Daddy! Gumdrop and I are best friends. I think she understands everything I say."

"Of course, she does. Gumdrop is a very intelligent horse. Be careful on the fence, honey. I don't want you to fall off. Do you think Gumdrop has exercised enough?" Bart asked, wrapping his arm around Rita's waist.

"Yes. We got tired," Rita answered with a yawn.

"Let's put Gumdrop back in her stall. It's time for dinner and bedtime for you and me," Bart said, helping Rita slide down to stand.

"Okay, Daddy. I promised Gumdrop a sugar cube. Is that okay?" she asked, leaning slightly against his solid body.

"I think Gumdrop would consider that way more than okay," Bart laughed as he took the mare's reins and escorted the two beautiful ladies into the barn.

CHAPTER 20

Waking the next morning wrapped in her handsome Daddy's arms, Rita smiled happily. She never would have imagined that she'd actually find someone like Bart, who was looking for the same type of relationship, and the attraction was mutually strong. Cautiously, she crossed her fingers, wishing that something wouldn't go terribly wrong in their relationship. Waking up each morning next to Bart would be a dream come true.

Pushing her attention from the still-sleeping man to test her memory, Rita tried to think back in time. There were still some fuzzy memories, but her brain seemed to be sorting itself back into order. She remembered standing in the poolhall, trying to figure out how to get away from her awful boss with no one else getting hurt. Her heart raced as she remembered how scared she had been.

Bart stirred against her. His blue eyes flickered open to look at her with concern. "You okay, Ritagirl?"

"I'm scared of that man," she confessed.

"We are going to be very careful to avoid him today, honey. I'll be with you all the time. Soon, he'll be behind bars, and you won't have to worry about him," Bart said before leaning in to kiss her sweet lips. He didn't have to ask who she was afraid of. He already knew.

He rolled back to look at the time. "Time to get up, Little girl. We need to be on the road in an hour." Bart flipped back the covers, letting the cool air wrap around them as he sat up.

Within a short amount of time, Bart had his Little girl dressed and fed. He'd allowed her to wear the freshly laundered clothes that she'd been wearing when she'd been injured except for the jeans. Those had been rejected for being too uncomfortable over her diaper. A pair of leggings from chest had taken their place. Those were super stretchy and relaxed. In fact, if Rita was perfectly honest, wearing her bra wasn't nearly as comfortable as she had been yesterday without it.

Starting to walk out of the house, Rita stopped just inside the door. "Daddy, can I go back to my room for a minute?"

"To the nursery?" he asked, lifting one quizzical eyebrow.

"Yes!" she answered simply and then squirmed as he continued to hold her hand. "I forgot something I want to take with me."

"Oh?"

"I just thought Zeebee might want to get some fresh air and sunshine. Those are important for zebras," she replied very convincingly.

"Zeebee, huh? Go get your stuffie. There's plenty of room in the truck for one Daddy, one darling Little girl, and one zebra who's risking rickets from a lack of sunshine," Bart said with a laugh.

"What's rickets?" Rita had turned to go back for her toy and then hesitated to ask the question.

"There's plenty of time on the way to the police station for us to discuss it. Go get Zeebee. Walk!" he ordered when she hesitated again.

At his strict command, Rita turned immediately and started walking. About halfway to the nursery when she was out of his sight, she stopped and stuck her tongue out at the handsome man. She didn't have to jump when he said so. Now smiling as she walked as slowly as possible back to her nursery.

When she got there, Rita decided that Zeebee would get cold without any socks. Opening a drawer in the dresser against the wall, she searched through the contents. No socks. Methodically, she slid each drawer open, taking her time as she looked for socks.

After several minutes passed, Bart called down the hallway, "Rita-girl? Did you get lost?"

Rita sniffed in indignation and went to sit on the floor next to the toy bin. She picked out a book and started to read it out loud to Zeebee and all his stuffie friends. She ignored the footsteps that came down the hall and just kept reading. "And all the mice ran quickly away from the big, black cat. They were…"

"Little girl. What are you doing? It's time to go," Bart said in a low tone that seemed to brook no monkey-business.

"I'm not going," Rita said, turning the page of the picture book. "Look, Zeebee! It's that mean alligator again. We don't like him."

"We are going! This is not a choice. We need to answer the police officer's questions so he can handle Eddie Shaffer and put him away, so you're not threatened by him. Stand up and grab Zeebee. We need to be on our way," he said firmly. A faint crease appeared between his eyebrows.

"No. I'm going to finish this book. You can never leave a book in the middle. That's like the law. You have to finish the story." She finally looked up at him with a distant air and added, "I may read another one after that." Rita sniffed loudly and turned back to her book.

"Oh, no, Little girl. That is not the way you want to talk to your Daddy," Bart warned.

When she looked up, Rita noticed that the crease between his eyebrows had deepened to a definite wrinkle. "You didn't talk nice to me. You barked an order at me. I don't have to do what you say." As she talked, that wrinkle became a crevasse.

Maybe I pushed too hard? That little voice in the back of her mind asked.

"The moment you called me Daddy, you put me in charge," Bart's tone didn't lighten. "Let's go, Rita. We have an appointment with Officer Hamilton."

"I'll be ready in a little while," she answered, looking back at the book. She tried to ignore Bart. Peeking from the corner of her eye, she saw him open the drawer under the changing table's padded top. He withdrew something that she couldn't quite make out. She saw him pick up a jar and begin to turn back to look at her.

Dragging her eyes back to the book, she began to read, "The alligator thrashed his tail…"

The book was firmly taken from her hand and closed with a snap. "What…?" Rita started to demand as Bart pressed her over to lie onto her tummy. With one hand pressing firmly into the small of her back, the large man held her securely against the carpet. His other hand stripped the clean leggings down over her hips. Her diaper was unfastened and whisked away.

"You can't spank me. You'll hurt my head," she reminded him.

"Little girl, you need to learn that Daddies have many ways to teach their Littles good manners," he said ominously, setting the shiny metal object onto the carpet in her view. It was contoured to be tapered at the tip and widen in the middle before narrowing slightly once again. It rested on a broad base.

"What's that for?" she asked in a trembling voice. She watched him open the jar of lubricant with one hand, and quickly she knew precisely what punishment he planned. Her bluster and anger had evaporated, abandoning her to her fate.

Tethered firmly to the soft carpet, Rita began to apologize. "I'm sorry. I shouldn't have ignored your instructions. I'm ready to go now."

"We'll be delayed just a few more minutes," he said, sliding the anal plug into the lubricant and scooping up a finger full of lubricant. His other hand released her for mere seconds to separate her buttocks slightly as his palm pressed against her tailbone. That finger of lubricant disappeared from her view.

"Noooo!" she wailed as that finger spread the cold lubricant over her most secret opening. Before she could take another breath to beg him to just give her a warning, that finger pressed inside her bottom. "Daddy! Daddy, no! I'll be good."

"I'm glad to hear that," Bart said, calmly. His finger didn't move inside her bottom. It just pressed deep inside.

Long seconds passed. "Please, Daddy?" Rita tried again, sure that she had been punished enough. To her relief, that finger glided back out of her bottom. That comfort only lasted a few seconds when, to her horror, she watched his fingers pluck the metal flange from the slippery lotion in the jar. "No, Daddy. I'm sorry."

"I know you are, Ritagirl," he said as he spread her buttocks just a bit further. "Relax your bottom. It will make it easier," he suggested before continuing to lecture her. "Little girls always need to test their Daddies. It's what they do."

Her eyes widened as the plug began to invade her narrow passage. "It's too big, Daddy."

"Relax. The plug will fit easily into your bottom. This is the smallest size. We'll work you up to larger sizes," he assured her.

"What? Why?" she demanded, turning to look over her shoulder at him. His eyes were focused on her bottom. Just how intimately he was looking at her, crashed over her body. *He's in total control,* she realized. Her head turned back to the front and drifted down to rest on her hands.

Her body went limp under his controlling hand as she drifted into a mindset that she'd never experienced. She heard his praise of "Good girl" as he pressed the plug slowly into her body. It's progression inside moving more smoothly as her resistance dropped. She moaned as the broadest section of the plug entered her bottom, and it slid into place with the wide flat section stopping its progress.

The plug dominated her thoughts and attention. Rita focused on the cold feel inside her. She felt her Daddy rub her buttocks fondly, slightly jostling the plug inside her. He shifted quietly beside her before he rolled Rita over and lifted her to sit on his lap.

She curled against his broad chest, clinging to him desperately. As he rocked her back and forth, she could feel the plug moving inside her body as a constant reminder that she was Little. The feel of his strong body against her gave her stability and reassurance.

He was her Daddy. The one she'd searched for throughout all her fantasies. Bart filled a hole in her life that she'd never expected to have completed. Minutes went by as he held her in his arms. Finally recovering, Rita kissed his muscle-corded neck.

"It's okay, Ritagirl. Daddy understands. Littles need to test their boundaries from time to time. Daddies should always be there to help guide them. I will always be there for you, Little girl," he promised.

"Are you sure you want me for your Little? I'm kind of a mess," she whispered.

"There isn't a doubt in my mind, Ritagirl. You are mine."

CHAPTER 21

B art maneuvered the truck through the heavy rush hour traffic with skill. His Little sat right next to his side. He patted her thigh lightly. "We're almost there. Are you ready to talk to the police officer?"

"Can you take this… thing out of me? You know, before?" Rita asked, looking up at him hopefully.

"No. You need a reminder that your Daddy loves you and that he's going to protect you," Bart said as if the plug was nothing more than a string wrapped around her finger.

"Do you think they'll know?" she worried.

"No one will know but you and me," he reassured her. His hand wrapped around hers as they twisted in her lap.

She looked up at him. Her mouth was pulled tight, almost obscuring her red lips. "I'm scared, Daddy."

"I know. It's going to be okay. We'll take care of making the official report now that you can remember what happened, and the police will pick Eddie up. Then, you won't have to worry about him at all," Bart reassured her as he pulled into the public lot next to the police station.

Parking the truck in the first available space, Bart reached over the seat to pull a jacket from the back. "Let's wrap you up a bit," he instructed, holding it up for her to slip her arm into.

"I'm not cold, Daddy," she hesitated. Her eyes widened as she realized that Bart wanted her to wear it more for concealment than for warmth. "You want me to hide?" she asked in a small, frightened voice.

"I want you to be safe. No one is going to hurt you. I will be right there with you," he promised as he helped her put on the oversized jacket.

Bart opened his door and went around to the passenger side to help his Little out of the truck. When her feet touched the pavement, she gasped slightly. His smile revealed he knew the plug inside her was making itself known.

"I'm never going to misbehave again, Daddy," she fervently promised.

Bart winked and wrapped his arm around her to sweep her away from the pickup. With a thud and a beep, he closed the door and locked it. Guiding his precious Little to the front entrance, Bart scanned the area. He didn't expect anyone to be stupid enough to approach them within feet of the entrance, but who knew?

Opening the door, he ushered Rita into the large building. The interior was industrial and free of any decorations or relief from the stark gray of the walls. They identified themselves at the desk and soon were met by Officer Hamilton. Bart apologized for their lateness as they walked back to the interview room.

Two hours later, the officer walked them back to the entrance. Although there were still a few blank spots in her memory, Rita's description of that awful night had been taped and transcribed. Officer Hamilton had put out a warrant for his arrest along with Eddie Shaffer's picture from the security cameras at the poolhall.

The warrant for Eddie's supplier included the words armed and dangerous. He had not been involved in Rita's abduction, but the police wanted to talk to him on suspicion of drug trafficking. He'd been identified as Carl Frennon and had two prior convictions for petty crimes. It looked as if he'd continued his life of crime.

When finally, Bart secured his Little's seatbelt in the truck and slid in beside her, Rita was exhausted, and her head was pounding. He drove to a deserted parking lot roughly three blocks from the police station. Parking with the passenger door facing a large privacy fence, Bart jumped out of the truck and came around to her side.

"What are we doing?" Rita asked as he unbuckled her seatbelt.

"I think that plug has served its purpose. Will you remember to listen to your Daddy from now on?" His eyes studied her face.

"Yes, Daddy! You'll never have to put a plug in my bottom again," she rushed to assure him. Looking around, she nervously questioned, "But here? What if someone sees?"

"No one will see," he assured her before reclining her seat and helping his Little roll over on her tummy. Quickly dispensing of her pants and diaper, Bart spread her buttocks widely to grasp the base that rested snuggly against her puckered opening. With a twist, he pulled it smoothly from her bottom and stored it in a plastic bag from the back. He'd clean it later.

Restoring her clothing, Bart helped her sit up as he raised the chair so she could look out the windshield. They were soon on their way back to SANCTUM. Her cute wiggles of relief in her seat made him smile.

With the plug removed, Rita's attention shifted. She leaned down to grab the handle of her purse that the officer had returned to her from the bar. The Little knew that she should send a message to her friends at the bar, but she couldn't focus. Using the excuse that her phone was surely dead anyway, she let go of the strap allowing the purse to drop to the floorboards.

Suddenly exhausted, Rita asked in a small voice, "Can I lie back down? I'll be really good," she promised.

"Let me get out of the city traffic, and we'll adjust the seat to let you lie back. Drink your water," he ordered, pointing to the bottle of water that she had been given at the police station.

"Yes, Daddy," she said with a smile breaking through the fatigue etched on her face. Unscrewing the top, she had a big drink.

"I love to hear that," he replied.

"I like to say it." Rita recapped the bottle and slid it between her thighs. Laying her head on his shoulder, she crashed into sleep.

CHAPTER 22

W hen they cleared the city traffic, Bart knew a car was following him. He'd noticed it behind him about a mile from the police station when it raced through a red light to keep following him. Unwilling to accuse an innocent driver of tailing them, Bart had turned back and forth through several side streets to make sure. Now outside the city, there was no doubt.

Reaching into his pocket, Bart dialed Doug Hamilton's cell phone. "Bart Jennings here. I have a battered blue sedan following me. There are two men in the front seat."

His voice woke Rita up. She turned to watch him with growing concern. He watched her peek over her shoulder at the car as he answered the officer's questions. Bart nudged her gently to signal her to turn back around. When the conversation finished, Bart slid the phone back into his shirt pocket.

"We're being followed. Officer Hamilton is dispatching cars in the area to converge on our location. Don't look back. If we're lucky, they'll just lurk back there until we're far away from the city. That will give the police time to catch up with us," he explained, monitoring the car behind them.

"I don't like this," Rita whined.

He could hear how nervous she was. "It will be okay, honey. The police are going to come for them. Here's what I want you to do. Get my phone from my pocket and find Mitch's number in the directory. Call him for me, Ritagirl," Bart instructed, giving her a job to do that would help distract her from the menace behind them.

"Put it on speaker," he asked softly as she tried to hand him back the phone. When it began to ring out loud, Bart murmured, "Good girl!" He returned the smile she flashed him.

"Hello," a deep voice answered the phone.

"Mitch? This is Bart. I've got a problem. First, let me tell you I have you on speakerphone, and Rita is sitting here in the truck with me," Bart warned his friend that the Little was listening. Mitch would know to buffer his reaction to keep the Little from getting more frightened.

"We're returning to SANCTUM from the police station, and I've picked up a tail. The police are sending cars, but I am quickly moving out of their jurisdiction. I wanted to give you all a heads up in case I'm bringing trouble back to SANCTUM. I'd like to invoke Operation Babysitter," Bart shared.

"Right away. Keep in touch. Let us know when you are a half-hour away," Mitch requested before disconnecting.

As she cleared the phone's screen, Rita hesitantly asked, "What's Operation Babysitter?"

"It's just SANCTUM jargon. Something for Daddies to know," he reassured her as he kept an eye on the sedan behind him. It wasn't gaining on the truck. He had a bad feeling that the men inside were simply waiting for the traffic to thin out a little further out of town to do whatever they had planned.

"Hold on to the phone for Daddy. You'll be my official caller, okay?" Bart hoped that having something to do would distract his nervous Little at least a bit.

CHAPTER 23

Rita was trying not to let her Daddy know how scared she was, but she knew she was failing miserably. She could see him looking back in the mirror frequently to check how close the car was to the truck. She wanted to look back, but Bart had told her to stop. Holding the phone tightly in her hand, she snuck glances at his face trying to read what was happening behind them from his expression.

The truck suddenly gained speed. She could see Bart's foot, stomping down on the gas pedal. She looked ahead and couldn't see anyone else on the now-abandoned highway in front of them. They were all alone. "Daddy, are we going to be okay?" she begged for reassurance.

"We're going to be just fine, sweetheart. I think I hear police sirens. Do you?" he asked as his hands glided the speeding truck over the road.

Closing her eyes to concentrate, Rita listened hard. She didn't hear them, but she trusted her Daddy. The Little crossed her fingers and began to wish as hard as she could. Her eyes flew back open at a cracking sound that came from behind her. Unable to resist, she twisted around to see the sedan right behind them.

"Get down on the floorboard, Rita," Bart ordered.

She flicked open her seatbelt and scrambled into the empty position in front of the passenger seat. Shoving the abandoned purse out of the way, she focused on Bart. Trembling with fear, she tried to make herself as small as possible in cramped space.

"What about you, Daddy?" she asked, only to scream as the back window of the truck exploded behind Bart's head. Rita threw her hands over her head for protection as shards of glass sprayed through the cab.

"Daddy, Daddy! Are you okay?" Rita scanned his body, looking for injuries. To her horror, a small rivulet of blood streamed down one of Bart's cheeks. She started to crawl from the floorboards but was riveted in place by her Daddy's look.

"You're bleeding," she cried.

He scooted down as low as he could in the driver's seat before reassuring her, "I'm okay. A few of the glass shards cut me a bit. Call 911, Ritagirl. Let's see if we can hurry the police up," he directed as he tried to maintain the truck's speed. No longer able to look at the rearview mirror to see the car behind him, Bart risked taking one hand off the wheel to adjust the side mirror to his new position. The sedan had moved to the other lane to come up along the truck's side.

"Please, we need help. We're being shot at on the highway out of town. You have to help us!" Rita said, urgently into the phone. As she listened to the dispatcher's questions, suddenly, she heard it. A faint sound of sirens coming toward them.

"Daddy! I can hear them!" she shouted to the handsome man who attempted to keep the truck ahead of the threat long enough for the police to reach them.

"I think they heard it, too. The car dropped back slightly," he exclaimed in relief. Then, they heard the crack of shots again from behind them.

Bang! The left rear tire exploded, jerking the truck to the right before it careened to the left. Rita watched her Daddy slid fully back into position behind the steering wheel as he struggled to hold the truck on the highway. The sirens wailed louder and louder. Unable to take time to look ahead, he thought he saw the flash of lights in front of him.

Forced to slow the truck down to avoid flipping it over, Bart pulled over to the side and stopped. Noting their reaction, the handsome man moved instinctively. Immediately, he unbuckled his seatbelt, and he threw himself over Rita's body to shield her from the men as the sedan slowed to a stop next to them.

Rita pushed against her Daddy's body, wanting him to hide from the bullets she knew were coming to get her. "No, Daddy. They just want me. I'll get out, and they'll let you go," she pleaded.

"Not happening, Little girl," Bart answered tersely as he listened to hear what was happening outside. Seconds passed like hours as they waited. A screech of tires came from outside.

"Get out with your hands held high!" an authoritative voice yelled in front of them.

"The police," Rita whispered. A glimmer of hope began to shine in her heart. She desperately wanted to see what was happening, but Bart didn't move. Minutes passed slowly as her ears strained to hear what was happening. They could hear the commands of several police officers ordering the men to throw their weapons from the car and then to get out with their hands held high.

A flurry of gunfire erupted. Rita huddled in terror under her Daddy's body. She could hear bullets thud into the truck and just prayed that none would make their way through the truck body. Two shouts of pain reached her ears, and she began to cry. What if they'd killed the police?

Finally, silence descended. Rita could only hear her sobs and the soft breathing of Bart above her. "Daddy, is it all over?"

"If you promise you'll stay right where you are, I'll look," he softly replied.

"I promise," Rita assured him. She felt his weight shift slightly as he raised his head to look out the window. The sight must have reassured him because he moved back onto the seat. "It's okay? They're not going to hurt us now?" she questioned as she wrapped a hand over his knee, needing contact with her Daddy.

"The good guys got here in time," Bart reassured her. "Hold on." He stripped off his shirt to lay it over the glass scattered on the seat. He reached a hand down to help her out of the small space that had kept her safe during the gunfire. "We're going to slide out of the truck on the far side to avoid the glass. Be careful where you put your hands," he warned as he guided her body sit on his shirt and maneuver out of the cab.

Once safe from getting cut, Rita launched herself into Bart's arms. She peeked through the window of the truck just long enough to see Eddie lying still on the ground and the other menacing man bleeding from his shoulder sitting in handcuffs next to the sedan that had followed them. Bart quickly turned her face away from the scene in front of the truck. Horrified by all the violence, the Little allowed her Daddy to pull her away from the scene. On the far side of the truck, she allowed him to cuddle her body against his bare chest with her face hidden.

Several minutes later, after the slamming of several car doors, a deep voice addressed them. "You all okay? Do you need any medical care?" he asked, observing the smears of blood on Bart's body.

"I think we're fine, Sheriff. The flying glass got me a bit when they shot out the back window. You got here in the nick of time. We owe you a world of gratitude," Bart said, extending a hand to shake the officer's hand.

Rita peeked over her shoulder to see a tall man with salt and peppered hair dressed in a uniform behind her. Impulsively, she turned to throw herself into the sheriff's arms, repeating, "Thank you, thank you, thank you."

"You're certainly welcome, Little girl. I wish I had gotten to you earlier," Sheriff Ben Underwood said, patting her back to comfort her. "I appreciate the hug, but I bet your Daddy needs to hold you. He looks like he was pretty scared."

Immediately, Rita whirled to throw herself back into her Daddy's arms. Processing the sheriff's words, she stiffened. *How did he know?*

Bart rubbed a soothing hand over her spine as he read her thoughts easily. "Ritagirl, it's okay. Sheriff Underwood has a beautiful Little girl himself. She owns a sweet shop in the closest town to SANCTUM."

"She's the sweetest Little I've ever met!" the sheriff boasted. "She also loves to make new friends. She'll be so jealous that I met you first."

"What's her name?" Rita asked, sliding to Bart's side to be able to see the tall man.

"Samantha," he answered with a fond smile. His face returned to an official look. "We'll look forward to getting to know you better, but now, I need to take your statement. Unfortunately, I'll have to separate you. Bart, I'd like to question your Little girl myself. Would you go with my deputy to answer his questions?

The two men's eyes met in silent conversation. Bart knew that the sheriff would treat his Little with kid gloves making the questioning as easy on her as possible. He nodded his agreement before kissing the top of Rita's head. "You stay here with the sheriff. I'm going to walk right over there with the deputy. Okay?" he asked her gently.

Rita battled her desire to stay in her Daddy's arms with the knowledge that she needed to give the police her statement. After a brief hesitation, she nodded her agreement. Smiling as her Daddy gave her another kiss and a fond pat on the bottom before he walked a short distance away to answer his own questions, she turned to the sheriff ready to get this over.

After what seemed like a million questions, the sheriff reunited her with Bart and said, "Do you have transportation back to SANC-TUM?" he asked the other man. The observant sheriff had seen him texting after the deputy had finished asking questions.

At Bart's nod, he continued, "I'll keep you updated on the proceedings. The coroner is here to take Shaffer away, and my deputy will take Mr. Frennon back across the county line. The city police are waiting to take him to the hospital for treatment before they process him for jail. I don't think he'll get out soon. There are several warrants out for his arrest."

With a tip of his hat, the sheriff turned to confer with his deputies. Looking at the bullet holes riddling the truck and its lopsided position on one battered rim, Rita looked up at Bart, "Can we drive the truck? How will we get back home?"

Bart smiled. "I'm glad you're ready to go back home, Ritagirl. We won't be able to drive the truck. That wheel and rim have had it. I'll have to call someone to tow it to the repair shop. If I'm not mistaken, someone will be here in just a few minutes to take us home."

He took advantage of their time alone to brush as much of the glass out of their hair and clothing. Bart had gotten the worst of the spray, but some small shards had reached Rita's position on the floor. He could shake his head and body quickly to rid himself of the most superficial bits of glass, but he didn't want his Little girl to do that with her head injury. Using the comb from her purse she'd abandoned in the truck, Bart had stroked through her soft hair as she leaned over before he'd carefully brushed off her clothing.

Before the police cars had even turned off their lights to begin transporting the men, a large SUV pulled up to the truck. Two men stepped out and shouted greetings to the sheriff who waved at them. Turning to the damaged truck, they both shook their heads.

"Sorry, we didn't get here in time to help. I bet you're ready to go home," the tall man with black hair peppered with silver commented as they approached. The men looked over the shot-up truck with a sad shake of their heads. No one wanted to think of a Little inside that vehicle.

"You have my thanks for being here now. Even if I could fix the tire, I don't know what else has been damaged. I'll have the mechanics look over it carefully before my Little gets back in that cab. We appreciate the ride home," Bart said, shaking their hands. His other arm remained wrapped securely around his Little girl. "Ritagirl, this is Greg Oldweiller and Josiah Davis. Josiah and his Little girl, Lindy, live at SANCTUM."

"Lindy?" she echoed, smiling at the two men. Even exhausted, she was thrilled to hear about the other Littles living SANCTUM.

"Lindy is my Little," Josiah answered. "She's very concerned about you. Priscilla told them how nice you are, and now the other Little girls are jealous that she got to meet you first. At the gathering this evening, all the Littles worried about you both. I'll be glad to tell her you are okay. How about if you pile into my car, and we'll take you back to SANCTUM? We'll arrange for someone to come pick up your truck later."

Five minutes later, Bart sat in the back seat with his Little stretched out on the seat with her head on his lap. Rita tried to stay awake, but the smooth ride of the truck and the murmur of the deep voices lulled her exhausted mind to sleep. She slept as soundly as a baby.

CHAPTER 24

S tirring on the soft sheets, Rita's eyes drifted open. She was so warm and comfortable that she considered going back to sleep, but then she remembered! "Daddy?" she questioned sleepily.

"Yes, Ritagirl. I'm right here," the familiar warm voice answered as the bed dipped down in front of her.

Last night, she had been barely able to keep her eyes open when the SUV pulled up in front of Bart's home in SANCTUM. Her Daddy had carried her into the house. After a shower to make sure all the glass was gone from her body and clothing, Bart had tucked the barely functioning Little into his bed.

"We're safe now, right?" she asked, pushing herself up to her knees to look into his eyes.

"Frennon is in jail. Sheriff Underwood texted to tell me that the charges against him are growing. They've searched his house and found illegal drugs and weapons. It doesn't look like he'll ever get out of jail. You may not even need to testify," Bart said as he wrapped a hand around her shoulder and pulled her forward to kiss her.

"Mmmm!" she murmured against his firm lips that pressed against hers so tenderly. Rita loved the taste of Bart's mouth. Warm and slightly coffee-flavored, she knew that he'd been up for a while. Lifting her lips, she said, "I'm sorry I've been such a lazybones."

"It was very late when we got to bed, honey. It was way past both of our bedtimes," he answered with a smile.

"Do you have a bedtime, Daddy?" she asked with a skeptical look. Surely Daddies didn't!

"I needed sleep, too. But you're right, I don't need as much as a Little girl. My job has me used to staying up for long hours. Animals don't get sick just during office hours," he said with a wink.

"Umm… Can I ask you a question?" she asked, plucking at the comforter that covered her knees.

"Of course."

"Are you still going to be a vet? If we live here and your office is back in town, how's that going to work?" she asked in a jumble of words.

"I have a partner in the city. We're going to rotate our care of the office. We'll go back to the veterinarian clinic every two weeks for a while to give her two weeks off. Meanwhile, I've already started helping an overworked country vet while I'm here," he patiently explained.

"I get to stay with you wherever you are?" she clarified eager to make sure that her Daddy wouldn't leave her in the city or in SANCTUM all by herself.

"I want you with me always, honey. Will you be okay being a vagabond and traveling back and forth?" he asked, watching her face carefully to judge her reaction.

"If I can be with you, I don't care where we are. Being together is the most important!" she declared.

"Give your Daddy a kiss, Ritagirl," Bart answered.

His voice dropped slightly, making her smile as she leaned in toward him. Rita had already noticed that her Daddy's voice lowered when he was aroused. She still gasped when he pulled her forward to hug her chest against his. When Bart took advantage of her open mouth to sweep inside in a pulse-raising kiss, she leaned against him fully and encircled his neck with her arms.

Bart's hands shifted to sweep under her nightshirt to caress her soft skin. Slowly, he pushed it up to her shoulder and then over her head. The Little shivered against him slightly as the cool air flowed over her body. She forgot about being cold when his lips captured hers again.

Holding her tightly against him, Bart distracted her with kisses as he unfastened the tape at each side of her diaper. When he lifted her slightly with one arm around her body to carry her back to lie on the mattress, she felt her diaper slide from her body. As soon as his arm loosened, the Little girl began to push his t-shirt up his muscled torso.

Bart was happy to oblige. His shirt flew across the room to land on the floor with hers. His hands began to explore her body as she wiggled in pleasure underneath him. The pleasure he brought to her body erased any embarrassment that she might have felt. Her hands roamed freely over his body as she tried to please him. The heat between them grew to an intolerable level.

With a groan, Bart ripped himself away from her caresses to stand by the side of the mattress. Quickly opening the drawer on the night-stand, he opened a sealed box of condoms and pulled one out to drop on the bed. As he rapidly unzipped the front of his bulging fly, Rita smiled at the thought that Bart had not made love with anyone else in this room. It was their private space.

She watched him, enjoying the sight of her Daddy as he removed his clothes urgently. Knowing that he wanted her as much as her body craved his was reassuring and arousing at the same time. Her eyes devoured his naked frame when he finally stood unclothed before her. Impulsively, she lifted the condom to hand it to this amazing man, watching the heat flare in his eyes at her eagerness.

"Open your thighs, Little girl. I want to see how wet you are," that husky voice commanded.

Shyly, she spread her legs apart, allowing him to see the glistening arousal fluid that coated her intimate folds and the tops of her inner thighs. When he breathed deeply to inhale the hot scent of her arousal, Rita could feel the wetness growing between her legs. His eyes fixed on the erotic scene in front of him as he rolled the condom over his thick shaft.

Deliberately, almost as if he was stalking her like prey, Bart loomed over her. He knelt between her thighs as his lips descended first to devour hers and then to press scorching kisses along her neck. One hand pressed into the mattress next to her to hold his body inches above her. She could feel the heat radiating from him and shivered at his desire.

When finally Bart fit his erection at her wet entrance, Rita arched upward to mesh their bodies fully. To her delight, her Daddy didn't continue to tease her. He glided slowly into her body, possessing her fully. When he paused, pressing deep into her tight channel, she began to beg for him to move.

"Please, Daddy. Please now!" she urged as her hip rose and fell underneath him.

"You are mine now, Little girl," he swore, capturing her eyes.

"Yes! Yes, Daddy. I'm yours!" she agreed with him, knowing that even a Daddy needed reassurance that her emotions echoed his.

"Wrap your legs around me, Ritagirl," he commanded. It was the only warning she received as he began to thrust fully into her body. Waves of pleasure crashed over their bodies, cementing their bodies and their future together.

CHAPTER 25

R ita felt suddenly shy. Priscilla's Daddy, Mitch, had invited everyone over for a welcoming party for the newest Little. There were so many new faces. She ducked slightly behind Bart's body.

Everyone knows I'm Little, she realized with a flash of embarrassment. They knew how he cared for her and that she was wearing a diaper he'd just started to make her use. Rita wasn't sure that she was ready for everyone to know all the embarrassing details of her life. *Maybe their Daddies don't ask them to be Little like mine does?*

Bart's arm reached around her shoulders and drew her out from her hiding spot. Leaning over, he whispered, "It's okay, Ritagirl. These people accept you for who you are - a precious Little girl."

She looked at him skeptically. A burst of laughter drew her attention over to her friend, Priscilla. Rita didn't like that she was laughing at her.

"Oh, don't get mad. I'm sorry. It's just that we had a bet," Priscilla pointed to the four women standing with her. "We wondered how long it would take you to look at your Daddy just that way. Like he was an alien from outer space speaking some kind of weird language. We don't understand them either some days."

The others nodded and smiled at Rita. Instantly the newest Little relaxed a bit. *Maybe they're really just like me?* Rita smiled back and immediately was surrounded by the Little girls who rushed forward to hug her.

Everyone was so excited to see her. They'd even put on nametags they'd decorated to help her learn their names. Priscilla, Shelby, Lindy, and Poppy all lived at SANCTUM all the time, but Samantha and her Daddy had come for the occasion as well. Rita peeked over her shoulder to look for the sheriff that had saved them from the two horrible men. He waved cheerfully with a big smile.

"When my Daddy told me he'd already met you, I was sooo jealous!" the full-figured Samantha informed her, stressing the one word to express just how jealous she had been. "Then, he told me you'd had bad guys after you. I'm sorry you met him that way. I'm glad I get to meet you at a party. Now, we get to have fun!"

"And Priscilla got to meet you and feed the new calves with you! I'm super jealous that I haven't gotten to see them yet," Shelby sent a reproving glance over at two men that stood together with the Daddies.

Beau noticed and replied, "I promise Shelby, tomorrow. Now that your tummy feels better after being cleaned out, you'll be able to enjoy seeing the new calves so much more."

Shelby's face turned a deep red color. She turned back to the Little girls who all huddled around her in sympathy.

"I hate enemas too, but I always feel so much better after Daddy treats my tummy," Lindy said in an embarrassed whisper.

Me too echoed around the group, and Rita knew that all their Daddies were as dedicated to taking care of their health as Bart was. She smiled at the Littles. "I'm glad to meet you. I was sure that I was the only Little in the world!"

"We all did! But we're not!" Poppy rushed to reassure her. "Come on. You need to make a name tag. Then, we'll introduce you to our Daddies, so you know who goes with whom."

"Then we'll make s'mores!" Shelby enthused.

"For dessert, Little girl. You have to eat your veggies and hamburger first," a deep voice came from behind them.

"Yes, Daddy!" Shelby agreed before turning back to the Littles. She leaned in and whispered, "They hear everything!"

"You have two Daddies?" Rita asked wide-eyed.

"Yes. It's wonderful… and dangerous for my behind," she winked at Rita. "Come on."

The Littles pulled Rita to a low table surrounded by chairs with short legs on the deck outside. Priscilla explained that it was her craft table where she colored and painted. She created beautiful things outside because "Daddy says glitter is dangerous inside!" They sat down to help Rita decorate her nametag. When it was proclaimed beautiful by all, Rita put it on with a huge smile.

Next, they escorted her over to the group of Daddies gathered around the barbecue grill. After all the introductions, Rita's brain couldn't remember everyone's name. When she looked to him with confusion apparent in her gaze, Bart added, "Rita is recovering from a concussion. She'll need to ask everyone's name a few more times before she'd be able to remember."

Rita beamed at him for understanding how she was feeling and making sure that everyone didn't think she was being rude if she didn't know their names. When all the Daddies decided that they needed to make nametags, the group of men moved over to the craft table. Sitting in the low chairs with their knees up around their ears made all the Little girls laugh. Their giggles continued when they watched the nametag creations that the Daddies were concocting.

Fun activities entertained the Littles as the badge-wearing Daddies began to put together the meal. Shelby taught everyone to make daisy chains, and they each made one for their Daddies to wear like crowns on their heads. They looked so silly as each Daddy tried to balance one on his head. Mitch ended up grilling his with the hamburgers when he forgot and looked down to flip the patties. By dinner time, they had all disintegrated.

Sitting on their Daddies' laps, the Littles ate until their tummies were bulging. No one thought they could eat another bite until Priscilla whispered the magic word, smores. Then, everyone could find room for one of the gooey desserts that had become a tradition at their cookouts.

With the last bite of her smore clutched firmly in her hand, Rita fell asleep on her Daddy's lap. Bart plucked it from her hand and chewed as the conversation of the men around the fire pit continued for another hour. The Daddies enjoyed getting together as much as the Littles.

Finally, it was time for everyone to return to their homes. Smoothly rising from their chair, the Daddies all said a quiet goodbye as they set off down the paths to their homes or back to trucks to drive home. Sheriff Underwood and Samantha's house was still in the construction phase. They would spend the night at Mitch and Priscilla's home.

The two remaining Daddies laid their Littles down for the night in Priscilla's nursery. A mattress on the floor served to cradle Samantha comfortably. A few minutes later, they met in the kitchen for a cup of coffee and some time to talk.

"Do you think Rita will have to testify against that scumbag?" Mitch asked with a scowl.

"No. I'm afraid he was targeted by a group of inmates in the city prison and killed. He'd escaped his last jail sentence by informing on the ringleaders of a large drug smuggling group. The warden had believed he'd be safe with the small population of felons waiting for their case to go to trial. Unfortunately, the communication links between inmates are more extensive than he realized. Carl Frennon was fatally stabbed in the showers," Ben informed him.

"I'm glad she won't have to go through that stress," Mitch commented after a pause.

"Me, too," the sheriff answered. The kitchen was quiet for a few minutes as they each considered the path that had brought each of the Littles to SANCTUM.

Finally, Ben mentioned, "I was interested to see that Greg Oldweiller came with Josiah to help Bart and Rita."

"Yes, he was here. He's been here a lot when we have loads of hay being delivered from the farm bordering SANCTUM to the east. Someday, we'll have enough men here full time to bale our own hay, but for now, we can buy it from a woman who lives next door," Mitch shared. "We all think she needs the money."

"And Greg's up here each time she delivers a load?" Ben asked with a spark in his eye.

"He is," Mitch answered with a big grin.

CHAPTER 26

Bart escorted Rita back to the bar to thank the waitresses who had reported her missing. The previous bar owner had repurchased the establishment from the bank when Eddie Shaffer's heir had defaulted on the loan. He'd profited greatly between the amount he'd sold the bar for and the cost to reclaim it. And he'd had a long vacation with his wife. He considered it a win-win, and all the employees were glad to have him back.

Those staff who had worked with Rita greeted her with hugs and lots of questions. Over a plate of her favorite bar food, nachos, and a tall glass of iced tea, Rita explained all that happened that night.

"Why didn't you yell? We would have helped you!" one waitress demanded with her hands on her hips.

"He had a gun and threatened to shoot anyone that intervened. It was better that I go with him so you all would be safe," Rita tried to explain.

"Next time, you yell," the waitress replied. Everyone agreed with nods and murmurs of agreement.

Rita looked at her friends and suddenly knew for certain she didn't belong at the bar anymore. When the next question came about when she'd be coming back, Rita looked over at Bart and smiled. Holding his beautiful blue eyes, she answered, feeling her heart moved up into her throat with apprehension, "I'm sorry. I'll miss you all so much, but I don't think I'll be coming back." Would he want her to stay in SANCTUM with him?

"Prince Charming is stealing you away, huh?" Marie, a fellow bartender, asked with just a hint of jealousy in her voice.

"I certainly am," Bart answered with a smile as he wrapped his arm around Rita to squeeze her tight.

T he Little girl and her Daddy had many serious conversations in the next coming months. Bart knew in his heart, she was his. He wanted her to be as sure as he was that she was his Little girl. In the back of his mind, Bart worried that she would choose to stay with him because she felt obligated or was afraid to live her life on her own.

"Daddy, stop asking me if I'm sure that I want to stay with you. If I hear that one more time, I will scream," Rita shouted at the breakfast table. They were discussing selling her furniture and giving notice on her apartment. Bart had been covering the cost of her rent as she recovered.

"Don't raise your voice to me, Little girl," Bart warned.

"AAAHHH!" she defied him with an ear-piercing screech.

Before her mouth even snapped shut, Bart unlocked the tray on her high chair. Plucking her from the seat, he draped her over his lap and began stripping off her pants.

"No, Daddy. I didn't mean to yell," Rita said, backpedaling to avoid a spanking.

Bart did not answer. His heavy hand came down on her pale skin, leaving a red handprint. As her voice rose again to a yell at him to stop, Bart smacked her bottom again and again until his Little girl laid sobbing over his lap. His hand gentled, rubbing over the fiery skin to soothe her.

He knew it would be easier for her to talk honestly without

looking at him. Caressing her punished bottom, he waited to hear the truth that he had been waiting for. Her arms wrapped around his calf, hugging him close to her body as her sobs diminished. Bart stifled a laugh as he felt her use his pant leg to wipe her tears away.

"Daddy? I'm sorry that I haven't told you the whole truth. I'm afraid that you only want me because you're guilty that I lost my memory jumping into your truck, and you feel that you need to take care of me," she admitted in the shuddering breaths still lingering from her sobs.

"I am very sorry that you got hurt in my truck," he said, lifting her curvy body to sit up now on his lap so he could look at her. "That is not the reason that I want you with me. I love you, honey. I love your Little side, and I love the strong woman that you are inside. I don't want to care for you because of guilt or feeling of obligation. I want to keep you with me forever because my life is happier with you in it. I've been looking for my Little girl forever. You are the one who I've been searching for. You complete my life."

He watched the impact of his heartfelt words register on Rita's face. A brilliant smile spread across her face chasing the red, blotchiness of her tears away.

"You love me?" she asked.

"I love you with all my heart, Ritagirl," he answered before leaning in to kiss her tenderly.

"I really want to stay with you. Can we get rid of all my stuff? I don't need it," she asked, holding his gaze steadily.

Bart knew that he'd erased her previously unspoken reservations. She was ready and able to make the decision that he'd been waiting to hear. "We'll go today to pick up anything that you'd like to keep, and then, I'll arrange for everything left to be sold. We'll put the money in an account for you to use however you wish."

Rita nodded happily. "Thanks, Daddy." She lifted her lips to offer them to him.

Kissing her deeply, Bart felt the final link click firmly into place. Now, they could enjoy the rest of their lives together. Lifting his head, Bart stood and tossed his precious Little over his shoulder before jogging down the hallway to their bedroom. She deserved a reward for finally telling him the whole truth. Listening to her giggles as he carried her through the house, Bart couldn't resist giving that enticing bottom a playful swat.

"Daddy!" his Little protested, giggling even more.

CHAPTER 27

Bart had finally declared that Rita could learn to ride Gumdrop. Her headaches had dwindled down to occur very infrequently. The motion didn't make her sick. He'd already warned her he'd pull her off Gumdrop immediately if she started to feel bad.

Rita had promised that she'd tell him the truth. The Little knew the consequences of lying to her Daddy. She'd earned two red bottoms already since Bart had decided she had recovered from worst of her concussion. The newest Little didn't know which she disliked most, a spanking or the anal plug. She sure didn't want to earn a punishment of both.

Dancing happily on the left side of Gumdrop, Rita chattered happily to her four-legged friend. "Hi, Gumdrop! I finally get to ride you. Isn't that great? You'll let me know if I'm too heavy, right? I don't want to hurt you?"

Bart had already assured his Little that her weight would not burden the strong, young mare. He pulled her close to him to kiss her lips. "You will not hurt Gumdrop, Ritagirl. Are you ready to step up into the saddle?"

When she nodded, he gave her instructions as he held on to her waist. "Put your left foot into the stirrup and hold on to the horn of the saddle. That's right. Good girl. Now step up on the stirrup." Bart helped lift her into the air. "Put your right leg over and sit in the saddle."

"Great job, Ritagirl!" he praised. "Can you put your other foot in the stirrup on the right side?"

He waited for her to smile and nod that she had her foot placed correctly. "Hold on to the reins," he instructed, handing them to her. "Remember not too tight. You don't want to hurt Gumdrop's mouth."

His Little had been determined to ride the beautiful horse throughout her recovery. Bart had taught her everything that he could in advance by setting a saddle on the top railing of the corral and letting her practice riding there. Leather strips attached to a post had served as reins to practice guiding the horse.

Holding onto the side of the bridle, Bart began to lead Gumdrop around the corral. Rita did an excellent job and looked at ease in the saddle. "You're doing great, Ritagirl. I'm going to let go, and you ride Gumdrop around the corral." Her smile widened as he stepped back from the bonded pair.

After a few minutes of circling, Rita asked on her next pass by Bart, "Can we go outside the corral? Just for a few minutes?" she begged.

"Go around a few more times while I get my horse saddled, and we'll go down to the creek and swim," Bart agreed with a smile.

"I don't have a bathing suit here, Daddy."

"We won't need one, Little girl," he answered before giving her a slow wink.

"Really?" she asked with pink tinged cheeks. When Bart nodded, she bounced in the saddle. "Let's go, Daddy." Her excited giggles filled the air as he jogged away to the barn.

As Bart saddled his horse, he remembered the day he had invested in the SANCTUM land. His dreams for the future had come true. Pulling his thoughts back to the present, he fit the bridle over his stallion's head. No need to dwell on past hopes, he had a Little to spoil.

The End

AFTERWORD

If you've enjoyed this story, it will make my day if you could leave an honest review on Amazon. Reviews help other people find my books and help me continue creating more Little adventures. My thanks in advance. I always love to hear from my readers what they enjoy and dislike when reading an alternate love story featuring age-play. You can contact me on
my Pepper North FaceBook page,
on my website at www.4peppernorth.club
eMail at 4peppernorth@gmail.com
I'm experimenting with Instagram, Twitter, Pinterest and MeWe. You can find me there as well!

For your reading enjoyment, my other age-play stories are:

SANCTUM

Pepper North introduces you to an age play community that is isolated from the surrounding world. Here Littles can be Little, and Daddies can care for their Littles and keep them protected from the outside world.

Sharing Shelby: A SANCTUM Novel
Looking After Lindy: A SANCTUM Novel
Protecting Priscilla: A SANCTUM Novel
One Sweet Treat: A SANCTUM Novel
Picking Poppy: A SANCTUM Novel

DR. RICHARDS' LITTLES

A beloved age play series that features Littles who find their forever
Daddies and Mommies. Dr. Richards guides and supports their efforts
to keep their Littles happy and healthy.

Zoey: Dr. Richards' Littles 1
Amy: Dr. Richards' Littles 2
Carrie: Dr. Richards' Littles 3
Jake: Dr. Richards' Littles 4
Angelina: Dr. Richards' Littles 5
Brad: Dr. Richards' Littles 6
The Digestive Health Center: Susan's Story
Charlotte: Dr. Richards' Littles 7
Sofia and Isabella: Dr. Richards' Littles 8
Cecily: Dr. Richards' Littles 9
Tony: Dr. Richards' Littles 10
Abigail: Dr. Richards' Littles 11
Madi: Dr. Richards' Littles 12
Penelope: Dr. Richards' Littles 13
Christmas with the Littles & Wendy: Dr. Richards' Littles 14
Olivia: Dr. Richards' Littles 15
Matty & Emma: Dr. Richards' Littles 16
Fiona: Dr. Richards' Littles 17
Oliver: Dr. Richards' Littles 18
Luna: Dr. Richards' Littles 19
Lydia & Neil: Dr. Richards' Littles 20
A Little Vacation South of the Border

Roxy: Dr. Richards' Littles 21
Dr. Richards' Littles: First Anniversary Collection
Jillian: Dr. Richards' Littles 22
Hunter: Dr. Richards' Littles 23
Dr. Richards' Littles: MM Collection
Grace: Dr. Richards' Littles 24
Tales from Zoey's Corner - ABC
Steven: Dr. Richards' Littles 25
Sylvie: Dr. Richards' Littles 26
(appears in the Dirty Daddies Anniversary Anthology)
Tami: Dr. Richards' Littles 27
Liam: Dr. Richards' Littles 28
Dr. Richards' Littles: 2nd Anniversary Collection
Tim: Dr. Richards' Littles 29
Once Upon A Time: A Dr. Richards' Littles Story

THE KEEPERS

This series from Pepper North is a twist on contemporary age play romances. Here are the stories of humans cared for by specially selected Keepers of an alien race. These are science fiction novels that age play readers will love!

The Keepers: Payi
The Keepers: Pien
The Keepers: Naja
The Keepers Collection

THE MAGIC OF TWELVE

The Magic of Twelve features the stories of twelve women transported on their 22nd birthday to a new life as the droblin (cherished Little one) of a Sorcerer of Bairn. These magic wielders have waited a long time to take complete care of their droblin's needs.

They will protect their precious one to their last drop of magic from a growing menace. Each novel is a complete story.

The Magic of Twelve: Violet
The Magic of Twelve: Marigold
The Magic of Twelve: Hazel
The Magic of Twelve: Sienna
The Magic of Twelve: Pearl
The Magic of Twelve: Violet, Marigold, Hazel
The Magic of Twelve: Primrose
The Magic of Twelve: Sky
The Magic of Twelve: Amber

Other Titles
    Electrostatic Bonds
    Perfectly Suited

AN INVITATION TO BE PART OF PEPPER'S LITTLES LEAGUE!

Want to read more stories featuring Zoey and all the Littles? Join Pepper North's newsletter. Every other issue will include a short story as well as other fun features! She promises not to overwhelm your mailbox and you can unsubscribe at any time.

As a special bonus, Pepper will send you a free collection of three short stories to get you started on all the Littles' fun activities!

Here's the link:

http://BookHip.com/FJBPQV

ABOUT THE AUTHOR

Pepper North is an indie author whose erotic romances have won the hearts of many loyal readers. After publishing her first book, Zoey: Dr. Richards' Littles 1 on Amazon in June 2017, she now has over forty books available on Amazon in four series. She is one of Amazon's Most Popular Erotic Authors, rising as high as 2nd in the top 100 and is a PAN (Professional Authors Network) member of the RWA (Romance Writers of America). She credits her success to her amazing fans, the support of the writing community, and her dedication to writing.

a amazon.com/author/pepper_north

BB bookbub.com/profile/pepper-north

f facebook.com/AuthorPepperNorth

O instagram.com/4peppernorth

P pinterest.com/4peppernorth

y twitter.com/@4peppernorth